YORK NOTES

General Editors: Professor A.N. Jeffares (*University of Stirling*) & Professor Suheil Bushrui (*American University of Beirut*)

Geoffrey Chaucer

THE MERCHANT'S TALE

Notes by Graham D. Caie

MA (ABERDEEN) PH D (McMASTER)
Senior Lecturer, English Department, Copenhagen University

  LONGMAN
YORK PRESS

YORK PRESS
Immeuble Esseily, Place Riad Solh, Beirut

ADDISON WESLEY LONGMAN LIMITED
Edinburgh Gate, Harlow,
Essex CM20 2JE, England
Associated Companies, branches and representatives
throughout the world

First published 1982
Tenth impression 1997

ISBN 0-582-03577-5

Produced by Longman Singapore Publishers Pte Ltd
Printed in Singapore

Contents

Part 1

Introduction

The life of Geoffrey Chaucer

It would be possible to give portraits of two Chaucers; the first is the Chaucer whom we come to know through his writings, a warm and human person, critical of the faults of his fellow men and his age, yet loving the sinner, though harsh on the sin. The other Chaucer is seen through the many official records we have of him as a civil servant. It is from this official documentation, which rarely mentions his literary output, that we can reconstruct a picture of his ancestry and career.

He was born in London around the year 1343, although the exact date is unknown. The name Chaucer comes from *chaussier*, meaning 'shoemaker', and implies French origins, but the family had been wine merchants back to the time of Geoffrey's grandfather, Robert. His father, John, a prosperous London vintner, held a minor court appointment and this tradition was continued by his son. Geoffrey is first mentioned in 1357 as a page to the wife of Prince Lionel, one of Edward III's sons, and it was then that he must have met the powerful Duke of Gaunt who was later to become his patron. Two years later we hear of Chaucer's capture in France during one of the expeditions that made up the Hundred Years' War. He was released the next year when Edward III paid part of his ransom. Although little is heard of him in the following seven years, it would appear that he was in Lionel's or Edward III's service on diplomatic missions abroad.

In 1366 he married Philippa Roet who was later to become the sister-in-law of John of Gaunt. She was employed at court in the service of the Queen. Chaucer also received an annuity from John of Gaunt and accompanied him on a military expedition to Picardy in 1369. In 1372 Chaucer travelled on the king's business to Genoa and Florence, and it is thought that this Italian trip was significant for him as a poet, for it is at about this time that we can see the Italian influence on his work.

From 1372 onwards there are innumerable documents that outline his career; for instance, his appointment as controller of the Customs on wool and hides in the port of London. This was no sinecure, so he appears to have been an active civil servant during the period of his literary career. He lived in a rent-free house in Aldgate from 1374 to 1388. Between 1376 and 1381 he was also employed on foreign service, presumably of a secret nature, visiting Flanders and Paris.

In 1386 Chaucer appears to have fallen out of royal favour. The young Richard II was now king and his advisor the Duke of Gloucester did not look favourably on any friend of John of Gaunt. Chaucer retired to Kent where he was Justice of the Peace and Knight of The Shire (equivalent to Member of Parliament), and it was in this period, about 1387, that his wife died.

In 1389 Chaucer was restored to favour and made Clerk of the King's Works. This meant being in charge of buildings and repairs in royal residences and parks. He gave up the position one year later, either because he had been robbed and beaten two or three times in a short period or because of the need to have time to write. His next appointment was as deputy forester of the royal forest in Somerset and in 1394 he was awarded a royal pension. It is generally accepted that he died on 25 October 1400 at the age of about fifty-seven; he was buried in Westminster Abbey where his tomb still can be seen.

From a literary point of view we should appreciate the fact that he was a member of the merchant class and a civil servant but had strong ties, through his position and his wife, with court circles. He was widely travelled in France and Italy, from where most of his literary inspiration came. It also appears that he was a loyal and trusted subject, favoured by three monarchs, Edward III, Richard II and Henry IV, and was given secret missions to fulfil.

From his literary works we can gather that he was well-read in philosophy and theology, a friend of Ralph Strode (*fl.* 1350–1400) the Oxford philosopher, and a friend of contemporary English poets such as John Gower (*c.* 1330–1408) and the French poet Deschamps (*c.* 1345–*c.* 1406). He was possibly also acquainted with Wyclif the religious reformer (*c.* 1320–84), who was another protégé of John of Gaunt. There is a chance that he could have met Boccaccio (1313–75) and Petrarch (1304–74) while in Italy; at least he was well acquainted with their writings. Chaucer was also a competent astronomer, as can be seen from his work *A Treatise on the Astrolabe* and the many astrological comments in *The Canterbury Tales*. But above all his literary works show him to be a shrewd judge of human nature and of his contemporary society.

Chaucer's works

The English language had undergone rapid changes in the latter part of the Middle Ages. The Norman Conquest of 1066, when William of Normandy invaded England, meant that French culture and traditions swept over the country and that French was the language of the new aristocracy, and thence of courtly literature. Poets of the twelfth, thirteenth and early fourteenth centuries in England found it difficult to adapt the romance verse technique to the English language and it was really not until Chaucer experimented with verse forms that English found its poetic voice. Chaucer mocks the typically bad attempts to write in a metre and technique inspired by the romance language in *Sir Thopas*, the tale Chaucer the pilgrim tries to narrate until forcibly stopped because it is so painful. His native English verse form was alliterative poetry, that is, front-rhyme verse, which had its origins in Germanic, especially Anglo-Saxon verse. Chaucer also mocks this type of versification, suggesting it is the rough metre of an uncultivated poet, by describing it as 'rum, ram, ruf'. Undoubtedly this alliterative tradition had survived at an oral level and was therefore the form of unsophisticated verse, but in the fourteenth century it was experiencing a fascinating revival, for instance, in *Sir Gawain and the Green Knight*. Because of his great contribution to the creation of successful verse forms in English Chaucer is called 'The Father of English Poetry'. Indeed he inspired all poets until the Renaissance when we once more find poets of his calibre.

All of Chaucer's works are in English and he translated into English two major works of the Middle Ages which also influenced his own poetry significantly—*Le Roman de la Rose* and Boethius's *De Consolatione Philosophiae*. This fact matters, because it was a time when much court poetry was still in French, the language of the aristo-cracy, the court and the government, while Latin was used by the Church, senior civil service and diplomats. Chaucer's friend and fellow poet, John Gower, wrote three major works, each in a different language because they were intended for different audiences: a courtly poem in French called *Mirour de l'Omme*, an intellectual one in Latin, *Vox Clamantis*, and a collection of stories akin to *The Canterbury Tales* in English, *Confessio Amantis*, aimed at a broader public.

Chaucer's literary career is generally divided into two periods: the period of French influence and his 'Italian' period, though such a distinction is too general. His early works include the translation in 1372–3 of *Le Roman de la Rose*, a twelfth-century poem by Guillaume de Lorris and Jean de Meun, and *The Book of the Duchess*, probably written in 1369 on the death of the wife of his patron, Blanche, the wife of John of Gaunt. All his early works are dream visions and the major theme is that of love: lost love and the victory over despair in *The Book of the Duchess*, success in love and the concept of good fortune in *The House of Fame* (*c.* 1373), the debate on the concept of courtly love in *The Parliament of Fowls* (in the late 1370s) and *The Legend of Good Women*, about faithful love. In the 1380s Chaucer completed his great work *Troilus and Criseyde*, about the tragic love of two young people; the same story inspired also a play by Shakespeare.

The Canterbury Tales

Chaucer's greatest work was written in the period 1387–92 and probably up to his death in 1400, although some individual tales may have been written earlier. We learn in *The General Prologue* that each of the approximately thirty pilgrims will tell two tales on the way to Canterbury and two on the return journey, but as there are only twenty-three tales we can guess that Chaucer's original purpose was never fulfilled. Yet the work does form a unity: *The General Prologue* provides an excellent introduction, presenting the characters and setting the literal and symbolic scene, while *The Parson's Tale* succinctly concludes the work. There are tales that are linked together by comments in their introductions and conclusions. These united groups of tales are usually called 'Fragments', but the final order of the fragments themselves is not absolutely certain. *The Merchant's Tale* must follow *The Clerk's Tale* and, as the Merchant alludes to *The Wife of Bath's Prologue* and *Tale*, we can assume that the Clerk-Merchant fragment follows the Wife of Bath-Friar-Summoner fragment.

The framework of the *Canterbury Tales* is of great interest. There was a tradition of collecting stories in the Middle Ages, as, for instance, in Boccaccio's *Decameron* and Gower's *Confessio Amantis*, so that Chaucer's collection is not so unusual. But the idea of a pilgrimage was a stroke of genius, as it gave Chaucer a unique chance to bring together people of both sexes, all social groups—aristocrats, merchants, artisans and peasants—and both clerical and lay people in a relaxed, holiday atmosphere. The pilgrimage gives those in closed religious orders a reason to leave their convent or monastery, and in no other setting could prioress and ploughman, knight and student, a cook, doctor and monk all come together and get to know each other. Here indeed is 'sondry folk' or 'God's plenty' as John Dryden (1631–1700) called them. Because of this very mixed group we find an equally diverse collection of literary genres, which again would have been difficult to bring together under other circumstances. These are a courtly romance (Knight), a tragedy (Monk), a beast fable (Nun's Priest), a sermon (Parson) and a number of 'fabliaux', popular, usually bawdy and humorous stories. The holiday atmosphere also means that the pilgrims, for instance the Wife of Bath and the Pardoner, will divulge more confidences than they would ever do in their home town. Furthermore, Chaucer has deliberately chosen to make his story collection as patriotically English as possible: the pilgrimage takes place on the way to Canterbury Cathedral from the Tabard Inn in Southwark, just south of London. The aim of this religious journey was ostensibly to visit the shrine of the English saint St Thomas à Becket who had been murdered in the cathedral in 1170 during the reign of Henry II.

Pilgrimages were very common in the later Middle Ages and for very different reasons. Some went for truly religious purposes, for instance, to do penance—that is, to cleanse themselves of a particular sin. Others were simply curious to see the relics or shrine, while many treated the journey as an excuse to go on a holiday in pleasant company and, especially, to be protected. The Wife of Bath, by listing all the pilgrimages she has been on for pleasure, makes it sound like the medieval equivalent of a guided tour abroad today. Thus we also see a moral cross-section of society (and indeed of humanity at all times). The fact that many are in religious orders does not make their motives and characters purer than the others. The broader implications of the pilgrimage technique can be seen when one realises that in the Middle Ages the pilgrimage frequently symbolised the journey of mankind through life. Egeus in *The Knight's Tale* says that 'this world nys [is not] but a thurghfare ful of wo,/And we been pilgrymes, passynge to and fro.' Chaucer's little society moves from the worldly inn to the cathedral, and the Church was considered a heaven-on-earth. The journey, therefore, is that of mankind who *ought* to move from worldliness to holiness. The good Parson at the conclusion of *The Canterbury Tales* hopes that with Christ's grace he can show his fellow travellers

> the wey, in this viage [journey],
> Of thilke [that] parfit glorious pilgrymage
> That highte [is called] Jerusalem celestial.

Chaucer, therefore, shows how people choose of their own volition to lead their lives; his microcosmic group reflects the macrocosmic society of mankind in all ages.

In *The General Prologue* we learn that the pilgrims meet at the Tabard Inn where the innkeeper, Harry Bailey, called the Host, offers to accompany them to devise entertainment. He suggests that each tells tales to and from Canterbury and the best raconteur will be rewarded with a free supper on their return. The Host provides useful links between the tales by introducing and summing them up, often in a brusque and crude manner. We cannot therefore accept his comments as Chaucer's, nor are we meant to see the authorial 'I' of *The General Prologue* as Chaucer's own voice, but that of Chaucer the pilgrim, who attempts to be an objective, impartial man who cannot even write good poetry. We must, therefore, be careful whenever the narrator intervenes and not automatically accept his comments as being Chaucer's own.

Another link between the tales is the overriding theme of love and the nature of love—love of God, love of mankind, erotic love, love of money, or of other worldly things. When we have been introduced to a pilgrim in *The General Prologue* and have read the tale he tells, we can begin to consider the teller and his motives. The tone of the tale and the interpretation the teller gives to it reveal his attitudes and his failings. It is in this way and in particular by the use of irony that Chaucer satirises the follies and evils of mankind; but, no matter how much he criticises the sin, his warm humanity shows through and his treatment of the sinner is generally mild. Chaucer is no harsh moralist or satirist, and we must always remember that he is as eager to entertain as to teach.

The Merchant in *The General Prologue*

In *The General Prologue* (so called to differentiate this introduction from the prologues to individual tales) Chaucer presents his characters in an apparently objective manner. He lets the 'I' character, Chaucer the pilgrim, describe their major characteristics. Frequently we can learn by what he *omits* rather than what he actually says; for instance, if he only mentions the dress, manners and demeanour of a character in holy orders we might assume that there is nothing to say about his or her devotional life. Here is the portrait of the Merchant:

> A Marchant was ther with a forked beerd,
> In motelee, and hye on hors he sat,
> Upon his heed a Flandrissh bevere hat,
> His bootes clasped faire and fetisly.
> His resons he spak ful solempnely,
> Souning alway th'encrees of his winning.
> He wolde the see were kept for any thing
> Betwixen Middelburgh and Orewelle.
> Wel coude he in eschaunge sheeldes selle.
> This worthy man ful wel his wit besette:
> Ther wiste no wight that he was in dette,
> So statly was he of his governaunce,
> With his bargaines, and with his chevyssaunce.
> Forsoothe he was a worthy man withalle;
> But, sooth to sayn, I noot how men him calle.

(There was a Merchant there with a forked beard, dressed in parti-coloured cloth [perhaps the livery of a guild], sitting high in the saddle. He had a Flemish beaver hat on his head and his boots were elegantly and well tied. He stated his opinions impressively [possibly 'pompously'], always proclaiming the increase of his profit. He wanted above all else the channel between Middleburg [Holland] and Orwell [Suffolk] kept safe. He was in the money exchange business [*sheeldes* = *écus*, French coins: such trade was illegal]. This worthy man used his intelligence [or 'cunning'] to the fullest: no one knew he was in debt, as his conduct in business affairs and money borrowing was so dignified. Indeed he was a worthy man moreover, but, truly, I don't know what he was called.)

The Merchant's portrait is the first of the commoners', immediately following those of the clerical characters. This suggests that he is socially highly considered. Our first impression of him is that of a fine figure of a man, sitting with dignity on his horse; he appears rich, wearing an expensive hat, and we may infer from his clothes that he is a member of the influential and wealthy merchant adventurers' guild. He stresses the need to keep law and order on the seas and puts forward his views impressively. Until this point the portrait is positive, but our suspicions are first aroused when we hear that he trades in French currency at a profit. This was illegal, as only royal money-changers could do it; but the main point is that he is not only in debt but conceals the fact. This was a common criticism of merchants in Chaucer's day, and such a pretence of wealth would have been frowned on more then than now. Thus our original image of the Merchant as a rich and successful businessman is shattered by this revelation. The unfavourable portrait is continued by the mention of *chevyssaunce*, money borrowing, which was also against the teachings of the Church.

The final two lines are confusing. Chaucer, repeating *sothe*, 'truly', says that he was a *worthy* man. Chaucer frequently uses this word ironically, and this is surely the case here. The apparently unnecessary statement in the last line that he does not know the man's name must be significant, as there are few pilgrims who are actually named. Chaucer could either have a particular merchant in mind and in this way invite us to guess his name, or he could be deliberately suggesting that this man who considered himself rich and influential was really insignificant.

The final picture is therefore one of duplicity (perhaps his two-pronged beard implies this, although it was in the fashion). The Merchant is a man who conceals the true nature of his condition. Such an impression fits the image we receive of him from his later performance. We know his true opinion of marriage from his Prologue, yet the 'hero' of the tale proposes the opposite view.

It is also significant that this portrait in *The General Prologue* is so short. We know little about him, other than his duplicity, so that we are left with the impression of a man whose life is entirely taken up with money, shady deals and the attempt to conceal his real situation.

A note on the text

Manuscripts of *The Canterbury Tales* date from very early in the fifteenth century and there are around eighty-three that have survived. They were copied, some beautifully illustrated and many with marginal glosses, all through the fifteenth century. The first printed text was made by Caxton in 1478.

The best complete edition of Chaucer's works is that by F.N. Robinson, *The Works of Geoffrey Chaucer*, second edition, Oxford University Press, London, 1957. There is an excellent critical edition of *The Merchant's Prologue and Tale* by Maurice Hussey, Cambridge University Press, Cambridge, 1966. Line references given in these Notes are to both these editions: R = Robinson's edition and H = Hussey's.

	Robinson	*Hussey*
The Merchant's Prologue	1213–1244	1–32
The Merchant's Tale	1245–2418	33–1206
The Epilogue	2419–2440	1207–1228

Part 2

Summaries

A general summary

The Merchant in the *Prologue* to his tale answers the Clerk, who has just completed the moral story of patient Griselda, by lamenting how miserable he finds the state of marriage and saying how he regrets getting married two months previously. He expands on the defects of his wife until the Host, Harry Bailey, asks him to tell a tale about marriage, as (the Host adds with tongue in cheek) the Merchant appears to be such an expert on the subject.

The tale is about an ageing knight called January, who lives in Lombardy. He had never been celibate, although a bachelor, but when he is sixty he begins to burn with the desire to be married. He praises the blissful state of wedlock, calling it a paradise on earth, especially if the wife is young and attractive and able to give him an heir. There follows a long passage, presumably by the Merchant himself, in which he supports the naïve January, condemns bachelorhood and lists the joys of marriage. Since we know the Merchant's real views on marriage, this section must be ironic. The Merchant quotes the Bible and other sources, and criticises all who attack this sacrament.

January summons his friends and asks their opinion. He gives his reasons for marriage on religious grounds, yet we can clearly see by the stress he places on the youthfulness and beauty of his potential bride that he is not only thinking of his soul. The brothers Placebo and Justinus argue for and against wedlock. Placebo simply reflects January's own views as he is a smooth-tongued courtier whose aim is to please. It is also evident that January's mind is already made up. Justinus, on the other hand, warns him against marriage by listing all the difficulties and dangers. Naturally January listens only to Placebo and sends his friends out to find the perfect girl and to arrange a speedy marriage. Once more such help is unnecessary as he finds a beautiful, young and tender girl himself. He recalls his friends, tells them of his success, dares them to contradict him and again stresses the advantages of marriage for his soul.

The wedding ceremony to May is hastily planned and briefly described by the Merchant, who dwells much longer on the feast and the events of the wedding night. January anxiously empties his house of guests as politely as possible. Damian, January's young squire, is now introduced and we are told that he too is infatuated by May's beauty. The scene of the wedding night is described in graphic detail: January's professed virility is contrasted with his pathetic performance, his taking aphrodisiacs, his physical repulsiveness and his roughness with May; and the self-confidence he claims as a dashing lover is contrasted with the laborious love-making of an old man.

Damian, meanwhile, becomes love-sick and dreams only of May, eventually plucking up courage to write her a letter which he is able to deliver when January asks his wife to visit the ill squire. May returns Damian's love and the narrator praises her for being so caring in her love. We are now introduced to the paradisial garden where January and his wife often make love.

Then tragedy strikes when January becomes blind. He greatly fears that May will be unfaithful. As he never leaves May for a moment, it is difficult for her to be with Damian, until she makes a plan. She has a copy made of the key to the walled garden and Damian uses it to slip in before the couple arrive. She pleads her faithfulness to January while she signals to Damian to climb a pear tree.

At this point two mythological characters, Pluto, king of the faeries, and his wife Proserpina, are introduced. Pluto is shocked at May's deception of the old man, preaches on the treachery of women, and vows to give January back his sight. Proserpina, however, defends May and women in general, and says that she will protect May by giving her a ready answer, should January's sight return.

May, meanwhile, complains of a pain, claiming to be pregnant, and has a desire to eat a pear. She gets her husband's permission to climb the tree (where Damian is) and stands on January's back to climb up, while January embraces the tree in case anyone else should climb it after her. At the critical moment of lovemaking between Damian and May, Pluto restores January's sight and the latter is naturally horrified by the vision of his wife's infidelity. May counters his outburst of indignation by claiming that she is responsible for the restoration of his sight, as the cure involves her 'struggling' in a tree with a man. She has only done it for January's sake. She also maintains that his eyes deceived him when first regaining sight and she scolds him for being so ungrateful. He finally believes that it is his eyes that have misled him and he kisses her in thanks.

In the *Epilogue* the Host concludes by agreeing with the Merchant about the deceits of women and reveals that he too has a wife with a 'heap of vices'.

Detailed summaries

The Merchant's Prologue: lines R. 1213–1244, H. 1–32

The Clerk's Tale of patient Griselda who obeyed her husband in every respect concludes with a false moral, jokingly added by the Clerk, that wives should let their husbands 'care, and wepe, and wrynge, and waille' (be anxious, weep, writhe and wail). This line is taken up by the Merchant, whose tale follows immediately, and he claims to know all about the misery of being a husband. He lists the evils of the wife to whom he has been married for only two months and laments his loss of freedom. He generalises about marriage, stating that for most husbands life is full of grief and anxiety. The Host asks him to say more about marriage. The Merchant agrees but says that he will not talk of his own marriage as it has hurt him enough already.

NOTES AND GLOSSARY:
In addition to the words and phrases included in these glossaries, a list of common, frequently occurring words is given on pages 64–5.

care:	anxiety
even and a-morwe:	in the evening and next day; night and day
trowe:	believe
I woot it fareth:	I know it is what happens to me
the feend ... were:	the devil were married to her
I dar wel swere:	I bet on it
yow reherce:	repeat to you
Hir hye malice:	her great spite
at al:	in all respects
Bitwix Griseldis ... pacience:	between Griselda's great patience. Griselda is the perfect example of a patient wife
passynge:	incredible
unbounden:	unmarried
also moot I thee!:	literally—as I hope to prosper; God help me!
I seye sooth:	I speak the truth
St Thomas of Ynde:	Doubting Thomas, who refused to believe in Christ's resurrection until he had felt his wounds. He was supposedly a missionary in India later
As for ... nat alle:	this refers to the majority [of husbands] but not all
shilde:	forbid
ywedded be:	been married
pardee:	truly
though that men ... sorwe:	even if tortured he couldn't tell of greater sorrow
for soory herte:	because of my wounded heart

The Merchant's Tale: lines R. 1245–1266, H. 33–54

The Merchant begins his tale by introducing his major character, January, a prosperous knight who lived in Pavia in Lombardy. (The location also suggests financial prosperity, because of the reputation of Lombard bankers.) January is a sixty-year-old bachelor who has always given free rein to his desire for women, but has now decided to marry, either because of religious reasons or senility. He prays to God to grant him the blissful life, the paradise on earth, which he considers marriage to be. Knowing what we do about the Merchant's attitude, the line 'Thus seyde this olde knyght, that was so wys' must be highly ironic, although the Parson in his tale compares marriage to paradise twice.

NOTES AND GLOSSARY:

Whilom: once

ther as ... appetyt: where his desire lay

As doon ... seculeer: as those fools who are laymen do (that is, not priests)

Were it ... dotage: if it were for religious reasons or senility

swich a greet corage: such a great desire

T'espien ... be: to search out a possible wife

ones: at the same time

hooly boond: holy bond (union). There is a pun with *housbonde* in the preceding line. As with *unbounden* (R. 1226) the Merchant subtly implies the binding, ensnaring aspect of marriage

first: in the beginning

so esy and so clene: so comfortable and so pure

Lines R. 1267–1310, H. 55–98

This section comprises the first part of a speech in praise of marriage which appears to be by the narrator. Its style is highly rhetorical and exaggerated, which suggests that the praise of marriage is insincere. Ironically, however, most of what he says would have been accepted by the Church, so that the narrator's scepticism rebounds on himself. The narrator, then, picks up January's sentiment and agrees that it is marvellous for an old man to marry a young girl who will give him an heir and be the 'fruit' of his wealth. He reprimands bachelors whose life is full of sorrow and insecure love. Marriage brings an ordered and happy state, especially as the wife will be obedient, faithful, and serve and care for her husband when he is ill. Some theological writers, however, warn against marrying, claiming that a servant would suit a man's needs better, is more economical and will not demand half his fortune; neither can a servant cuckold a man (that is, deceive her husband by having a lover).

NOTES AND GLOSSARY:

sooth:	true
namely:	especially
hoor:	white-haired
feir:	a fair one
solas:	delight
it sit wel:	it suits well
brotel:	brittle, insecure
wene sikernesse:	imagine safety
bryd:	bird
arreest:	restrain (arrest)
estaat:	position
ordinaat:	well-ordered
yok...ybounde:	bound in this yoke of marriage
habounde:	abound
buxom:	obedient
trewe...ententyf:	faithful and also so attentive
syk and hool:	in sickness and health
make:	mate
wele or wo:	for better or worse
nys nat:	is not
bedrede:	bedridden
he Theofraste...tho:	that [famous] Theophrastus is one of them. Theophrastus (c. 372–286 B.C.), a Greek naturalist and philosopher, was the author of an anti-matrimonial work, *The Golden Book of Marriage*
What force...lye:	what does it matter if it pleases Theophrastus to lie?
for housbondrye:	for economical reasons
dispence:	expenditure
good:	goods, possessions
verray:	true
knave:	manservant
hoold:	keeping
Ful lightly...cokewold:	you can very easily be made a cuckold (deceived by your wife being unfaithful)
sentence:	opinion
ther God...corse:	may God curse his bones
take no kep...vanytee:	do not pay attention to such illusions
Deffie...me:	defy Theophrastus and listen to me

Lines R. 1311–1361, H. 99–149

The narrator continues his praise of marriage, having rejected Theophrastus's anti-matrimonial teaching. A wife is God's gift to be prized above all worldly things; she also lasts longer—perhaps longer than you would like (and this comment would certainly appear to be from the Merchant himself). He then launches into a rhetorical sermon on the holy sacrament of marriage which was created in paradise so that Woman could help Man. As she is so virtuous and obedient they are as one being. A wife helps a poor man work, never contradicts him and does all he asks. With exaggerated praise the narrator glorifies marriage and urges all wedded men to praise God for their wives. If a husband only follows the wife's advice he will never go wrong.

NOTES AND GLOSSARY:

yifte:	gift
varraily, hardily:	truly, certainly
commune:	common property
moebles:	movable possessions
drede:	fear
Wel lenger ... paraventure:	longer than you would like, perhaps
I holde him shent:	I consider him ruined
seculer estaat:	not in the clergy (priests would be expected to be unmarried)
ywroght:	created
bely-naked:	completely naked
terrestre:	terrestrial, worldly
disport:	pleasure
They moste nedes lyve:	they simply have to live
o:	one
wele:	prosperity
Seinte Marie:	Saint Mary—Mary, mother of Christ
benedicite:	bless us! (pronounced *bénsitáy*)
Certes:	Surely
bitwixe hem tweye:	between those two
swinke:	work
never a deel:	nothing at all
lust, ... weel:	wishes, she likes very much
nat ones:	not once
murye:	pleasant (merry)
halt hym ... leek:	considers himself worth anything
sikernesse:	security
gesse:	believe
So that ... reed:	if he follows his wife's advice

Lines R. 1362–1392, H. 150–180

There follows a series of biblical examples, supposedly to illustrate the narrator's argument that wise men follow their wives' advice. (Yet on closer inspection it can be seen that these wives in fact betrayed men.) Jacob and his mother Rebecca, Judith and Holofernes, Abigail and Nabal, Esther and Mordecai are used as examples. A number of popular proverbs about marriage follow and the long speech concludes with orthodox religious views which compare the husband-wife relationship with that of Christ and his Church.

NOTES AND GLOSSARY:

Lo!:	For instance. A common rhetorical device to introduce examples like these.
Jacob:	Rebecca tricked her blind husband Isaac into blessing her son Jacob instead of Esau. As Esau was a hairy man she tied kid skin onto his hands and neck to deceive the blind husband. (See the Bible, Genesis 27:6ff.) Such an example of a wife deceiving a blind husband is fitting in this tale, but does not support his argument
clerkes rede:	priests advise
conseil:	advice
mooder:	mother
his fadres . . . wan:	he won his father's blessing
Judith:	in the apocryphal biblical book of Judith, chapters 11–13, occurs the story of Judith who freed the children of Israel by deceiving and then killing Holofernes
kepte:	preserved
Abigayl:	in the biblical book of I Samuel 25:14ff. Abigail saved her husband Nabal who had angered King David. On Nabal's death David married her
Ester:	in the biblical book of Esther, Chapter 7, Esther helped to promote her cousin and protector Mordecai at the court of the King of Persia, Ahasuerus (Assuere), whom she later married; and she also protected the Israelites from persecution. All the women mentioned used their charms to achieve their ends, not always to aid their husbands
enhaunced:	promoted
in gree superlatyf:	superior in degree
Senek:	Seneca, the Roman author. In fact this thought is ascribed to Albertano

Suffre:	Endure
Catoun bit:	Cato bids. Dionysius Cato, author of the *Distichs*, a book of moral precepts
of curteisye:	out of courtesy
Ther as . . . kepe:	where there is no wife to keep house
wolt wirche:	will act
as Crist . . . chirche:	it was common to compare Christ's love for his Church with the husband's love of his wife. The narrator wishes us to compare this theoretical state with reality as he portrays it later
thee:	prosper
what so . . . pleye:	no matter what people say in jest or fun about it
namely . . . syde:	especially on the wife's side. An ironic remark, suggesting that the wife always gains more out of marriage

---

Lines R. 1393–1468, H. 181–256

The Merchant now returns to his story. January calls his friends to ask their advice about his plan. He claims that he needs to marry in order to save his soul from damnation, as he has been lecherous until then. However, the description he gives of his envisaged bride—beautiful and young—and his desire to marry immediately makes one wonder if he has only his soul in mind. He asks his friends to help him to find such a young girl, whom he describes in terms of tender meat to be savoured. Women of thirty are not so tasty, in addition to being too difficult to handle, too clever and experienced, whereas young girls can be controlled and moulded like wax (later we shall see how young May moulds wax to make a key and thus deceive January!). He would probably commit adultery if he were married to an older woman; and as he would have no legitimate children, his inheritance would go to strangers. He maintains that people who talk of marriage know no more about the subject than his squire; this is ironical because neither January nor the Merchant has much idea about the subject and because his squire, Damian, is more attractive to May than January is.

Again January falls back on religious reasons for marriage: to have children, to avoid lechery and to help each other, living like brother and sister. But, adds January, interrupting his theological discourse, although I am old I am still sexually active and could not live in such a holy union (thus confirming the fact that he uses religion and marriage as an excuse for continued lechery). Given the climax of the story, involving the pear tree, his comment that with his white hair he is like a tree with white blossom which is just about to give fruit, is highly ironical.

NOTES AND GLOSSARY:

inwith his dayes olde: in his old age

lusty: joyful

To tellen ... entente: to tell them what his intentions were

sad: serious (*not* 'sad')

hoor: hoary, white haired

on my pittes brynke: at the edge of my grave (at death's door)

folily despended: spent foolishly

mayde: maiden, girl

shapeth: prepare

al sodeynly: immediately

I wol fonde t'espien: I will try to seek out

mo than I: more (in number). There are more of you than me, you are more likely to find such a thing (that is, a wife)

and where me best ... allyen: and whom would be best for me to marry

ful fayn: very eagerly

pyk: pike. Pike are better to eat than pickerel and veal is better than old beef. This stresses his animalistic approach to marriage

bene-straw: old straw which can only be used to make a bed for beans

forage: cattle fodder

wydwes: widows. Possibly a reference to the Wife of Bath

They konne ... craft: they have as much skill

Wades boot: the source of this allusion is much disputed. It implies skill, possibly magical power

So muchel broken harm: so much harmful suffering (the phrase is also much debated)

whan that hem leste: when they want to

sondry scoles ... clerkis: different schools make a scholar skilful

gye: control

I wol noon ... cause: I do not wish to have an old wife precisely for this reason

For if ... myschaunce: for if it should be that I had such misfortune

plesaunce: pleasure

avoutrye: adultery

were me levere: I would rather

I dote nat: I am not being foolish (or senile)

my page: young servant (ironical, as young Damian is his young servant and proves knowledgeable in such matters)

chaast: chaste (a virgin)

Take hym a wyf: let him take a wife
leveful procreacioun: lawful procreation (reproduction)
for paramour: for love-making
leccherye eschue: avoid lechery
yelde hir dette: pay their marriage debt. See the Bible, I Corinthians 7:3 'The husband must give the wife what is due to her, and the wife equally must give the husband his due'
meschief: trouble
I dar make avaunt: I make bold to boast
my lymes...bilongeth to: my limbs strong and capable of doing all that is expected of a man
blosmeth...bee: blossoms before fruit has grown
As laurer...sene: as the laurel can be seen throughout the year
syn...entente: since you have heard my intentions

Lines R. 1469–1593, H. 257–381

January receives conflicting advice from his friends and an argument begins between the two brothers, Placebo and Justinus. Placebo, whose name means 'I shall please', praises January's wisdom and advises him to do whatever he thinks best. As a courtier he has always agreed with his lord, and his policy is to echo his superior's views. Justinus, whose name means 'Justice', provides a more outspoken and critical view. He advises January to consider very closely before bestowing his goods and his person on anyone else. There are many matters to consider and this takes time; he should check if she is wise, sober, proud, scolding, rich and so on. All you can hope for, says Justinus, is a wife with more virtues than vices. He himself (like the Merchant) has suffered much in marriage, although everyone praises his choice of wife. But beware of marrying a young girl, Justinus continues, now you are old. Even a young man would have difficulty in satisfying her.

January, however, totally rejects Justinus's advice and accepts Placebo's. His imagination runs riot as he sets about visualising his future wife. He enjoys himself viewing all the girls nearby: some are beautiful, some gracious and others rich but with a bad reputation.

NOTES AND GLOSSARY:
ensamples: examples
As...disputisoun: as differences of opinion always come amongst friends who dispute
cleped: called
Conseil to axe: to ask advice
sapience: wisdom

weyven fro:	to neglect
Salomon:	King Solomon. King of Israel, son of David (974–937 B.C.). He is traditionally a wise king
Wirk...conseil:	do everything advisedly (from the apocryphal biblical book Ecclesiasticus 32:19)
shaltow...thee:	you will not regret it
So wysly:	as certainly as
taak this motyf:	take this suggestion
court-man:	a courtier
stonden...estaat:	been in very high standing with lords who are very highly placed
kan:	knows
·semblable:	similar
wit:	knowledge
heigh sentence:	noble opinion
Ytaille:	Italy
Crist :.. apayd:	Christ would have been satisfied with this advice
heigh corage:	very courageous. *Corage* can also imply sexual potency; see line R. 1759, H. 547
stapen in age:	advanced in years
by my fader kyn:	an exclamation. Literally, 'by my father's kindred'
Youre herte...pyn:	you are in high spirits
Senek:	Seneca, the Roman philosopher and dramatist (*c.* 5 BC–AD 65)
Seith...avyse:	says that a man should consider very closely
catel:	goods
avysement:	consideration
assent:	opinion
Wher she be:	if she is
dronkelewe:	alcoholic
shrewe, chidestere:	ill-tempered, a scolder
mannyssh wood:	mad about men, very lustful
Al be it...in al:	even though no man can find anyone in this world that is right in every respect
if so were...badde:	if it so happened that she had more virtues than vices
this axeth leyser:	this requires time
Ful pryvely:	privately
cost, care, observances:	expense, sorrow, duties
route:	large number
eek the mekeste...lyf:	also the meekest alive
But I woot...sho:	but I know best where the shoe pinches
Ye mowe...do:	you may, as far as I am concerned, do just what you please

Avyseth yow: consider well
By hym: by God
route: company, gathering
To han his wyf allone: to keep his wife to himself
doon hire ful plesaunce: completely satisfy her
yvele apayd: ill pleased
Straw for thy Senek: I don't care for your Seneca
I counte nat ... : I don't pay attention to a load of scholastic terms
assenteden: agreed
letteth matrimoigne: hinders marriage
whanne hym ... wolde: when he wanted and with whomever he wished
Heigh ... bisynesse: wild imaginings and eager anxiety
gan ... impresse: began to make an impression
As whoso: like someone who; the mirror image stresses the distance from reality and the fact that it is only exterior appearances that interest him
commune: public
Thanne: then
Gan Januarie ... devyse: January began to contemplate in his mind
He wiste nat ... abyde: he did not know which girl to dwell on
stant so ... hath she: was considered in such a way by public opinion because of her seriousness and her graciousness that she was the most popular

---

Lines R. 1594–1688, H. 382–476

Without any help, January soon chooses a young and beautiful girl called May, 'for love is blind', the narrator ironically tells us. He dotes on her image, in particular her physical attributes. He calls his friends back again to tell them he has made up his mind and is not to be swayed by other arguments. She is not of high rank, but this beautiful girl will help him live a holy life and he will keep her all to himself. (January wrongly assumes that marriage excuses one of the sin of lechery.) He has one problem, though: he has heard that one cannot have bliss both on earth and in heaven. As marriage is so paradisial, can he risk losing the joys of heaven later? Justinus, who despises such nonsense, jestingly answers that perhaps God will perform a miracle and make his marriage a purgatory, a state of punishment; then he will go directly to heaven when he dies. Justinus continues on a serious note: marriage is not the paradise January expects. One must lead a moderate life not centred on erotic love, if one wishes to avoid sin. All one needs to do is to listen to the views put forward by the Wife of Bath who knows all about marriage.

NOTES AND GLOSSARY:

apoynted hym on oon: he settled on one [girl]

chees ... auctoritee: chose ... authority

blynd: January's later blindness, apart from its dramatic function, is symbolic of his lack of wisdom

purtreyed: portrayed

myddel smal: slim waist

governaunce ... gentillesse: demeanour ... noble character

sadnesse: seriousness

he on hire ... condescended: he had decided on her

Hym thoughte ... so badde: he thought everyone else's views so bad

fantasye: delusion

instaunce: request

abregge hir labour: shorten their work

Nedeth namoore: they no longer needed to walk or ride (in search of a wife)

He was ... abyde: he was resolved about his choice of wife

alderfirst ... boone: first of all he asked them all a favour

which that of beautee: whose beauty

Al were ... degree: even though she was of low social status

To lede in ese: in order to live a life of pleasure

han hire al: possess her completely

wight: person

nede: matter

shapen ... spede: see that he would not fail to be successful

reherce: mention

ful yoore ago: a long time ago

han parfite blisses two: have two perfect blisses

the synnes sevene: the Seven Deadly Sins which, according to medieval theologians, were Pride, Envy, Anger, Sloth (laziness), Avarice, Gluttony and Lechery

ese and lust: pleasure and delight

agast: afraid

delicat: delightful

For sith ... deere: since true heaven is reached with such difficulty. The Merchant considers all things in terms of purchasing. He believes that heaven can only be reached if one suffers during life. He is thinking of the idea of penance whereby the priest, after one has confessed one's sins, will suggest some kind of act that shows that one is repentant. Penance will thereby avert punishment in Purgatory. The act of repentance might involve prayers, financial contributions, etc.

bretheren tweye: two brothers or friends
Assoilleth me: explain to me
anon right in his japerye: immediately [replied to] his stupidity
auctoritee allegge: quote authority (that is, the Bible)
of his hygh myracle: by a great miracle
so for yow wirche: so bring it about for you
er ye have youre right: before you have received the last rite, that is, the sacrament after one's final confession before death
And elles . . . sengle man: or else may God forbid that He should send a married man grace to repent (implying punishment) more frequently than a single man
reed I kan: advice I know
Paraunter: perhaps
purgatorie: purgatory, the place or state in which souls after death are purged of sin before entering heaven. There is ironic play on the terms heaven, purgatory and hell throughout the tale. The Merchant considers marriage hell, January thinks it heaven, Justinus hopes it will be purgatory, Pluto is god of Hades (hell), etc.
Goddes meene: God's instrument
lette: hinder
So that . . . attemprely: as long as you use the joys of your wife moderately, as is reasonable. January thinks that lust in marriage is permitted, but Justinus points out this error
my wit is thynne: my knowledge is limited
But lat us . . . mateere: let us leave this subject
The Wyf of Bathe: The Wife of Bath is another character on the pilgrimage who has told a tale about how wives can use marriage to accumulate wealth from old husbands and how to dominate men
Fareth now wel: all the best to you, farewell

Lines R. 1689–1794, H. 477–582

The marriage treaty is hastily drawn up, May agrees, and she is endowed with January's property. (Again it is only the financial aspects of 'buying' her that are mentioned.) The marriage ceremony itself is briefly described but longer is spent on the wedding banquet which is exaggeratedly compared with great events in classical mythology. The drink, food and entertainment are described as well as the beauty of May and the eagerness of January to make love to her.

January tries to hurry the guests out of his house as he contemplates his virility and the events to come. All the guests are joyful except Damian, January's young squire, as he has also fallen in love with May. The narrator then launches into a lofty and rhetorical speech on treacherous servants.

NOTES AND GLOSSARY:

Han take hir leve:	they have taken their leave, each from the other
it moste nedes be:	it had to be
They wroghten so ... tretee:	they contrived by such a skilful and wise agreement
Mayus highte:	called May (implying the young, fruitful year)
I trowe ... tarie:	I fear it would delay you too long
scrit and bond:	deed and bond
feffed:	endowed
hooly sacrament:	the holy sacrament of marriage
Sarra and Rebekke:	Sarah and Rebecca. These two Biblical women are mentioned in the marriage service as representing faithfulness and wisdom. Rebecca has already been mentioned in connection with *deceiving* her husband (R. 1362, H. 151)
orisons:	prayers
as is usage:	as is common, customary
croucheth hem:	blesses them with the sign of the cross
And made ... hoolynesse:	and made everything sufficiently safe with holiness. The religious part of the wedding is narrated with hasty tempo and this line suggests the use of religion to condone January's lust and as a guarantee for salvation in spite of his use of his wife
solempnitee:	ceremony
deys:	daïs, the raised table
vitaille:	food
swich soun:	such sound
Orpheus:	the mythical musician, son of Apollo, who enchanted all nature with his music. He descended into hell for the sake of his wife, Eurydice
Thebes Amphioun:	Amphion, King of Thebes, was said to have aided the construction of Thebes by his music
Joab:	Joab, leader of David's army in the Bible, 2 Samuel 2:28: 'Then Joab sounded the trumpet ... and the fighting ceased.'
Theodomas:	an augur of Thebes whose invocation to the besieged Thebans was supposedly followed by a trumpet call

in doute:	in danger
Bacus...aboute:	Bacchus (the Greek god of wine and revelry) liberally pours wine for them all
Venus:	goddess of love; her laughter at the marriage of such unlike people is ambiguous. It implies that January had given himself up entirely to sensual love
assayen his corage:	test his ardour. The blazing torch Venus brandishes suggests burning love—the same that will smite Damian (see R. 1777, H. 565)
Ymeneus:	Hymen, the god of marriage
Hoold...pees:	be quiet
Marcian:	Martianus Capella, the fifth-century author of the Latin work *The Marriage of Philology and Mercury* (the marriage of language and wisdom)
Muses:	the Nine Muses were patronesses of the arts in Greek mythology
To smal...mariage:	your writing and rhetoric (that is, poetic talent) are too insignificant to describe this marriage
witen:	realise
it semed fayerye:	it seemed magical
Queene Ester:	Esther entranced King Ahasuerus by her beauty, but she did so in order to promote the Jewish cause and her relation Mordecai. See the Bible, Esther chapters 2 and 5. This, then, suggests ulterior motives in May's looks. (See R. 1371, H. 159)
devyse:	describe
gan...to manace:	threatened
in armes...streyne:	would constrain her in his arms
Paris, Eleyne:	Paris the Greek abducted Helen of Troy, thus causing the Trojan War. Here it implies sexual vigour and constraint. January sees himself as a virile young lover carrying off his beloved
But natheless...moste he:	but nevertheless he was very sorry he had to be violent with her that night
corage:	desire
agast...susteene:	afraid you will not be able to endure it
woxen:	become
were ago:	had gone
savynge his honour:	preserving his honour (that is, as politely as possible)
To haste hem...wyse:	to hurry them diplomatically away from the meal
that resoun was:	when it was correct to

squyer:	squire, a young 'trainee' knight, January's servant. Squires are frequently associated with amorous play. Hussey points out that St Damian was patron saint of medicine and it is ironical that he should be credited with the return of January's sight
Which carf:	who carved at the knight's (January's) table, the normal duty of a squire (see the *General Prologue*, R. 100)
That for . . . wood:	because of the great pain (of his love) he had practically gone mad. This is the typical, exaggerated behaviour of the courtly lover
he swelte and swowned:	he died and fainted
As that she bar it:	which she held
bedstraw:	mattress (straw used to stuff mattresses). This highly rhetorical speech expounds the dangers of harbouring a treacherous servant
famulier foo:	intimate enemy
hoomly hewe:	domestic servant
naddre:	adder
thy borne man:	a man borne to serve you

Lines R. 1795–1865, H. 583–653

The approach of night is described in a lofty, rhetorical manner, deliberately too elevated in style for such a tale, and contrasts with the following picture of the lover, January, drinking a good dose of aphrodisiacs to boost his desire artificially. He hurriedly empties his house of guests, goes through the ritual of having the priest bless the marital bed and at last is alone in bed with May, 'his paradise'. The narrator now concentrates on the love-making scene and highlights the disgusting features of January with the sharp bristles on his face scratching May's tender cheek. January apologises for his roughness and slowness, but a good workman needs time, he says. As they are married nothing they do together is sinful, he incorrectly claims, just as one cannot hurt oneself with one's own knife. After a night of hard labouring he starts to sing and croak and is in high spirits, chattering away with the slack skin around his neck shaking. God only knows what May thought about this performance, is the narrator's comment. She is obliged to remain in her apartment for four days, as was the custom.

NOTES AND GLOSSARY:

Parfourned . . . diurne:	the sun has performed his daily semi-circle. A rhetorical way of saying it was sunset

No lenger ... th'orisonte: no longer may his [the sun's] body remain on the horizon

rude: rough

lusty route: joyful gathering

Where as ... leste: where they do whatever they wish to do

sye hir tyme: see that it was time

hastif: hasty

ypocras, clarree, vernage: hippocras, a cordial drink; clarree, a drink of wine, honey and spice; vernage, a strong sweet white wine. These are aphrodisiacs which are supposed to strengthen sexual powers

t'encreessen his corage: to increase his desire

letuarie: medicine

daun Constantyn: an eleventh-century monk and physician of Carthage who wrote *De Coitu*; 'daun' is a title of respect

To eten ... eschu: he was not averse to eating all of them

privee: close

Lat voyden: empty

devyse: ordain

the travers ... anon: the curtains immediately drawn

as stille as stoon: as silent as a stone. This suggests the passivity and perhaps reluctance of May

yblessed: the blessing of the bed by the priest, like the drawing of the curtains, was a common tradition

dressed: made ready

make: mate. (Note that she is called 'his paradys' here)

brustles: bristles. This section with its realistic detail is deliberately repulsive and contrasts with the earlier, romantic picture implied by referring to classical lovers

houndfyssh: dogfish. Sandpaper-like skin, 'as sharp as briar'

I wol doun descende: I will go (down) to sleep

be doon at leyser parfitly: be done perfectly in a leisured fashion. He excuses his slowness by stating that things cannot be done well and quickly

It is no fors: it does not matter

In trewe ... tweye: we two are united in true marriage. His view that a husband can never sin with his wife is theologically incorrect; compare the illogical statement that one can never hurt oneself with one's own knife

gan dawe: dawned. *Gan* indicates the past tense

sop: bread dipped in sweet wine

wantown cheere: unruly behaviour

coltissh:	energetic, like a colt
ragerye:	passion
ful of jargon . . . pye:	chattering away like a spotted magpie
chaunteth . . . craketh:	sings and croaks. The imagery makes him look ridiculous and stresses his animalistic instincts
She preyseth . . . bene:	she does not think much of his fun. The silence and passivity of May are strongly contrasted with January's behaviour
pryme:	prime, 9 a.m.
Heeld hire chambre:	kept to her room. A tradition [*usage*] for newly wed brides, to show their modesty
For every . . . reste:	for every labourer must have rest sometime
no lyves creature:	no creature alive; *lyves* is an adjective here

Lines R. 1866–2020, H. 654–808

Our attention now focuses on the love-sick Damian who, burning with desire, eventually plucks up courage and writes May a letter which he keeps near his heart. May now leaves her room on the fourth day and joins January. When January hears of Damian's illness he suggests that she should visit him, praising Damian for being noble, discreet, trusty and manly. May visits Damian immediately and he secretly gives her the letter which she later reads in the lavatory and then disposes of it. May has now fallen in love with Damian even though he is poor, and the narrator effusively praises her nobility of mind for condescending to love him. She replies to Damian that he has only to fix time and place and she will submit to him. A delighted Damian rises from his sick-bed, preens himself and joins the company again.

NOTES AND GLOSSARY:

sely:	unhappy, poor
Andswere . . . cas:	answer my question on this matter
thy wo biwreye:	your sorrow reveal
sike:	sick
brenneth:	burns; compare the firebrand of Venus in R. 1777, H. 565
in aventure:	at risk
prively . . . borwe:	he secretly borrowed a writing case
compleynt or a lay:	a lament poem or a song
The moone . . . glyden:	the moon, which at noon on the day January married May was in the second degree of [the astrological sign of] Taurus had now glided into [the sign of] Cancer. This is another rhetorical device, apparently out of place in such a tale and refers to the few days May remained in her room

entendeth nat ... me: does not attend on me
how ... bityde: what does this mean
letted: prevented
That me forthynketh: I am sorry about that
harm and routhe: great pity
secree: trusty. We are forced to compare January's opinion of Damian with the latter's later actions
thrifty: of good service
bountee and ... gentillesse: kindness and nobility of spirit
taak good hede: listen
after-mete: after dinner
Dooth hym disport: give him pleasure
Have I no thyng ... lite: after I have just had a little rest
spede yow faste: hurry up
marchal: master of ceremonies
streight hir wey yholde: went away immediately
bille: letter
siketh ... depe: he sighs very deeply
Mercy: thank you
discovere: expose
kyd: known
ful softe: very quietly
feyned ... neede: pretended that she had to go where, you know, everyone has to go
She rente ... caste: she tore it into pieces and quietly threw it into the closet
studieth: contemplates
He wolde ... plesaunce: he wished, he said, to have some pleasure from her
be hire lief or looth: whether she wished it or not
But lest ... wrooth: but in case fastidious people are angry with me. Again the narrator's silence implies May's disgust
evensong: evening prayers (vespers)
by destynee or aventure ...: by 'destiny or chance, the power of influences or the natural outcome or the conjunction of the stars in the sky' (Hussey, p. 94)
to putte a ... werkes: to petition for the work of Venus (love)
deme: judges. Another attempt to raise the tone of the tale and imply divine intervention. All astrological speculation is unnecessary to explain the love between Damian and May
holde my pees: keep quiet
ese: pleasure
Certeyn ... noght: indeed, I do not care who is displeased by this deed

Lo, pitee . . . herte: see how compassion immediately flows in noble hearts

franchise: generosity

narwe avyse: closely contemplate

han lat . . . place: have let him die on the spot

verray grace: true favour

lakketh noght: nothing was omitted

his lust suffise: satisfy his desire

sotilly . . . threste: stealthily thrust

harde hym twiste: firmly shook his hand

al hool: completely recovered

He kembeth . . . pyketh: he combs his hair, makes himself neat and adorns himself

gooth . . . bowe: bows as low as a dog waiting to pounce on his prey. (*for the bowe:* 'waiting for the prey shot by the bow and the arrow')

craft: skill

lete . . . nede: leave Damian about his business

Lines R. 2021–2124. H. 809–912

Believing that true happiness comes from pleasure, January has among his other treasures a beautiful walled garden of delight. The King and Queen of the Faeries, Pluto and Proserpina, enjoy themselves there, and January makes love to May there in the summer. January alone keeps a key to open this paradise. The narrator launches into a rhetorical and emotional condemnation of the fickleness of fortune which has now made January blind and causes him great sorrow and jealousy in case his wife is unfaithful. January insists that she stay close beside him always. May weeps bitterly at being confined in this way and separated from Damian who is equally depressed, although they are able to make signs to each other. May takes a wax impression of the key to the garden and Damian has a second key made.

NOTES AND GLOSSARY:

Somme clerkes . . . delit: some scholars consider that happiness is found in delight. (An epicurean philosophy of sensuous pleasures)

as longeth: as is expected

Shoop . . . deliciously: he arranged to live in great delight

as honestly . . . degree: as appropriate to his social status

woot I . . . nowher: I do not know anywhere else

Romance of the Rose: The thirteenth-century French romance *Le Roman de la Rose* that Chaucer had translated. The action takes place in a Garden of Love

devyse:	describe
Priapus:	the god of fertility—with associations of natural growth in the garden and sexual drive. The Garden of Love setting is common in romance poetry and has associations with Eden, thence with the Fall, for instance, in *The Franklin's Tale*
laurer:	laurel tree
he Pluto:	Pluto in classical mythology was the god of the underworld. He dragged Proserpina down to Hades where she spent half of every year. She is therefore goddess of spring and fertility. There is a strong parallel with January and May; *he Pluto* implies 'that famous Pluto'
al hir fayerye:	all her following of fairies
disporten hem:	play
deyntee:	delight
no wight . . . hymself:	allow no one to keep the key except himself
smale wyket:	narrow gate
clyket:	key. The words *wyket*, *clyket* are onomatopoeic and repeated twice later. It implies that January alone had the key to May's affections
unshette:	unlocked
dette:	debt
spedde:	accomplished
O sodeyn hap!:	Oh unforeseen occurrence! This long speech in an elevated style in which Fortune is blamed for the loss of January's sight is ironic. January has been inwardly blind all along
envenymynge:	poisoning
brotil . . . queynte:	brittle joy, sweet yet deceptive poison
yiftes . . . stidefastnesse:	gifts with the colour of steadfastness
moore and lesse:	the great and the insignificant
biraft:	taken away
free:	noble
woxen:	become
So brente . . . fayn:	his heart burned so [with jealousy] that he wished
Ne wolde . . . wyf:	he did not wish her to be mistress or wife
Soul as . . . make:	alone like the turtledove that has lost her mate
aswage:	lessen
Save . . . forgoon:	except, doubtlessly, he could not prevent himself
benyngnely:	graciously
outher dyen . . . leste:	either die suddenly or else have him as she desired
privee signes:	secret signs

fyn: conclusion

For as good . . . se: for just as blind people can be deceived, you can be equally deceived when you have your sight. This summarises a major moral in the story

Argus: the hundred-eyed giant in Greek mythology was deceived and killed by Hermes (Mercury)

poure or pryen: gaze or peer

blent: blinded

wenen: think

Passe . . . namoore: it is a relief to pass on. I shall say no more

emprented: took an impression of

countrefeted pryvely: copied secretly

Som wonder . . . abyde: a marvellous event will occur concerning this key, if you wait

---

Lines R. 2125–2218, H. 913–1006

Ovid was right in stating that lovers would always get together by some trick or other. One fine day January has the strong desire (after May has encouraged him) to go with May to his walled garden where he can make love to her in the bushes, and he addresses her in a parody of the biblical Song of Solomon. Damian enters before them and hides in the bushes, while the blind January preaches to May about being faithful in marriage, because of the love of Christ, her honour and the inheritance she will gain from him. She earnestly promises to keep her wedding vows to remain true and argues that it is only men who are unfaithful; she is indignant that he need even mention the subject. As she says this, she signals to Damian to climb a pear tree.

NOTES AND GLOSSARY:

Ovyde: the Roman poet, Publius Ovidius Naso (43 BC–AD 17). His *Metamorphoses* contains the love story of Pyramus and Thisbe

ful sooth seystou: what you say is very true

What sleighte . . . manere: Love will contrive all things somehow, no matter how cunning, long or dangerous a trick she uses

kept ful longe . . . overal: constrained everywhere for a very long time

rownynge: whispering

Thurgh eggyng . . . wyf: by his wife's urging

turtles voys: the voice of the turtle dove. This passage is a parody of the biblical Song of Solomon, chapters 2 and 4. In the Middle Ages it was interpreted as referring to the love of Christ for his Church

dowve: dove

eyen columbyn: dove-like eyes
spot: harm
disport: pleasure. There is a discordant mixture of biblical and secular love all through this passage
lewed: ignorant. The effect of the beautiful biblical poetry is undercut by the narrator who discards the speech as 'ignorant'
stirte: went
clapte to: shut
Levere . . . offende: I had rather die on a knife than be violent with you
chees: chose
Beth to me trewe: be true to me
heritage . . . tour: inheritance, town and tower
chartres: deeds
er sonne reste: before sunset
wisly: truly
wyte me noght: do not doubt me
elde: old age
of my wyfhod . . . flour: this tender flower of my wifehood
Whan that . . . bond: when the priest bound my body to you
sterve: die
empeyre: injure (impair)
drenche: drown
wenche: common woman
And wommen . . . newe: and women always are reproached by you men
make: mate, husband
how he werchen shal: how he should act
pyrie: pear tree

Lines R. 2219–2319, H. 1007–1107

The scene shifts to the supernatural characters Pluto and Proserpina who come to the garden during this beautiful weather. Pluto launches into an attack on treacherous wives and he expounds the evils of women, taking Solomon as an example; he will help January to regain his sight and thus see May's treachery. Proserpina, however, takes May's side and says that she will aid May by giving her, and every woman thereafter, the ability to talk her way out of any situation. Even though the evidence is clear, women will be able to give a bold-faced excuse. She claims that in biblical and Roman history there are many examples of faithful women, while Solomon was a lecher and idolator. Pluto makes peace with his wife after this outburst, although both will keep their promises regarding January and May.

NOTES AND GLOSSARY:

blew the firmament: the sky was blue

Phebus...Ysent: Apollo, the Sun, has sent down his golden rays

Geminis...Cancer: the astrological signs of Gemini and Cancer

declynacion: 'the moment of least influence' (Hussey, page 99)

exaltacion: in astrology, the position in which a planet exerts its strongest influence

Jovis: Jove's (Jupiter's)

bifel: occurred

ravysshed out of Ethna: Pluto, in Greek mythology, abducted Proserpina while she gathered flowers near Etna

Claudyan: a version of this story is in the fourth-century author Claudius Claudianus

How...fette: how he carried her off in his terrifying chariot

turves: turf

no wight...nay: no one can deny

Salomon: see page 23

Fulfild of sapience: greatly endowed with wisdom

To every wight...kan: to all who have knowledge

Jhesus, *filius Syrak*: Jesus, son of Syriac, the supposed author of Ecclesiasticus. The mythological Pluto quotes biblical sources!

but seelde reverence: but rarely with reverence

ayen...syght: his eyesight again

vileynye: evil

harlotrye: wickedness

Bothe in repreve...mo: both to her own shame and that of others

by my moodres sires soule: by the soul of my maternal grandfather (Saturn)

in any gilt ytake: caught sinning

hemself: themselves

And bere...accuse: and overcome by arguments those who would accuse them

Al hadde...yen: although the man had seen something with both his eyes

visage it hardily: put on a bold face

as lewed as gees: as ignorant as geese

what rekketh me: what do I care

preved hire constance: proved their constancy

geestes: tales

ne be nat wrooth: do not be angry

sentence: meaning

in sovereyn bontee...she: in supreme goodness there is no one, neither male nor female, except God

Pardee ... ydolastre: truly, as much as you whitewash his reputation, he was a lecher and a worshipper of idols. The story is in the Bible, 1 Kings 11

lost his regne ... wolde: lost his kingdom sooner than he wished

I sette ... vileynye: I do not care a whit about all the evil

nedes moot ... breke: I simply have to speak or else my heart will swell to breaking point (I'll explode if I don't speak my mind)

sithen ... jangleresses: since he said we were gossips

As evere ... vileynye: as ever I intended to retain the tresses of my hair intact, I will not refrain, not for politeness' sake, from speaking evil of him who means us (women) harm

Dame ... it up: Madam, do not be angry any more, I yield

it sit me noght: it is not fitting for me

contrarie: oppose

Lines R. 2320–2418, H. 1108–1206

We now return to January, May and Damian who is up the tree. May claims to have a pain and wants a pear to cure it, implying that it is a desire in pregnancy. January laments the fact that no servant is nearby to get a pear for her. She makes January put his arms around the tree while she steps on his back and climbs up. In that way no one can climb up after her while she has momentarily left January. Immediately Damian and May make love in the tree, whereupon Pluto restores January's sight. He sees what is happening in the tree and roars with anger. But May cleverly talks her way out of the dilemma, claiming that she and Damian were performing an elaborate cure for January's blindness which involves a man and woman 'struggling' in a tree. January is still not totally convinced. May argues that when a blind person's sight is first restored he cannot see properly. She then turns the tables on January, accusing him of being too suspicious. January apologises for slandering his wife, they kiss, become friends and return home.

NOTES AND GLOSSARY:

ful murier than the papejay: merrier than a parrot

aleyes: garden paths (alleys)

An heigh: on high

sheene: radiant

Gan for to syke: began to sigh

I moste ... see: I must have one of the pears I see

so soore longeth me: I have such a great desire

for hir love ... queene: for the love of the Queen of Heaven (Mary). In fact May is aided by the Queen of the Underworld

in my plit:	in my condition (implying pregnancy)
no fors:	no matter
vouche sauf . . . to take:	agree to embrace the pear tree. May knows January does not trust her, but if he embraces the tree no man can climb it. Damian, of course, is already up the tree
Certes . . . :	Of course, I'll be pleased to help
twiste:	branch
I kan nat glose:	I cannot pass over [this event]
rude:	simple. The narrator pretends that it is outside his power to omit the crude details
throng:	thrust
Ne was . . . fayn:	never was there anyone so glad of anything
dressed:	directed himself, served
up he yaf a roryng:	he let out a roar
As dooth . . . dye:	as the mother does when the child dies. This is probably a reference to the popular Mystery Play, *The Slaughter of the Innocents*, when the mothers scream as Herod's soldiers kill their sons
harrow!:	help!
O stronge . . . dostow:	O hard and bold lady, what are you doing?
what eyleth yow!:	what is the matter with you?
holpe:	helped
to heele with youre eyen:	to heal your eyes
algate:	entirely
God yeve . . . dyen:	may God give you both a shameful death
swyved:	copulated
yen:	eyes
hals:	neck
Ye han . . . sighte:	you had a glimpse but not a perfect view. May regrets that her 'cure' cannot be perfect; if it had worked perfectly he would not have seen what he claims to have seen!
me thoughte . . . so:	I thought he was doing it to you. Now January lets a note of doubt enter
Ye maze . . . see:	you are confused . . . This is the thanks I get for making you see
kynde:	generous
my lief . . . apayd:	my dear, and if I have said anything wrong, God help me, as I have been ill-rewarded
I wende han seyn:	I thought I saw
wene as yow lest:	think what you like
taken keep:	grasp
adawed verraily:	properly awake

yse:	see
ysatled be:	has settled down
Beth war:	beware
mysdemeth:	misjudges
clippeth:	embraces

The Epilogue: lines R. 2419–2440, H. 1207–1228

The Host, Harry Bailey, expresses horror at the subtle wiles of women and completely agrees with the Merchant about wives' deceit. He mentions his own nagging wife and regrets marrying her, but does not say too much in case one of the pilgrims tells her later.

NOTES AND GLOSSARY:

Ey! Goddes mercy!:	may God help us!
oure Hooste:	Harry Bailey, who acts as master of ceremonies
tho:	then
sleightes and subtilitees:	cunning and tricks
sely:	poor
And from . . . weyve:	and they will forever deviate from the truth
labbynge shrewe:	babbling, gossiping wretch
Therof no fors:	but it is of no importance
But wyte . . . teyd:	but do you know what? In secret I greatly repent that I am tied to her
and I sholde rekenen:	and if I were to recount
ywis . . . nyce:	I would be very foolish indeed
meynee:	company (presumably he has the gossiping Wife of Bath in mind)
Syn wommen . . . chaffare:	since women know how to spread such affairs
eek my wit . . . tellen al:	and also I am not capable of telling everything

Part 3

Commentary

Chaucer's Merchant

Chaucer's aim in *The Canterbury Tales* is to show us a cross-section of humanity with all its flaws, follies and attractions. He does this by letting his naïve narrator, Chaucer the pilgrim, describe the characters, and then he lets the individual pilgrims present their tales without direct comment except from fellow travellers. They unwittingly tell us much about their true nature by their choice of tale and the tone and emphasis conveyed, as well as by their personal interpretation of the story.

From *The General Prologue* and *The Prologue to the Merchant's Tale* we glean the facts that the Merchant pretends to be rich when in fact he is in debt; that he is an eloquent speaker who makes impressive statements; that he has been married for only two months, yet hates marriage and blames his wife for his miseries. He also seems to lack wisdom, as seen in the way he misinterprets the preceding tale by the Clerk (see page 46). He is the first of the non-aristocratic laymen to be presented in *The General Prologue*, where the characters are introduced in hierarchical order. It is therefore implied that he is considered of high social standing, yet he tells a 'fabliau', a coarse story associated with 'churls', low characters (see page 43). He does not even gloss over the cruder details concerning sexual intercourse as does the churlish Miller who uses euphemisms. Yet the merchant does try to dress up his bawdy story in the trappings of a wise debate. The long initial debate on marriage with all its apparently profound statements is irrelevant to the story and appears to be an impressive façade for a morally shabby tale. In the same way January tries to blind us with theology and morality, when in fact he simply wishes to possess a beautiful young girl.

The Merchant's 'hero' is a senile knight who innocently enters what he considers the blissful state of marriage. But January is a man of straw, a caricature of a naïve male, the typical old lover of medieval literature who is invariably deceived by his young wife. Only a senile fool, the Merchant implies, could think marriage is bliss. By making January so naïve he must also be ridiculing himself, as he has just made the same mistake. If one does not see through January's grossly selfish reasons for marriage, one might well be lulled into believing, as the

Merchant undoubtedly wishes us to, that *all* wives are like May and that *all* marriages prove to be a hell-on-earth for the unsuspecting husband. And this is exactly how the hen-pecked Harry Bailey interprets the tale at the conclusion:

> Lo, whiche sleightes and subtilitees
> In wommen been. For ay as bisy as bees
> Been they, us sely men for to deceyve,
> And from the soothe evere wol they weyve;
> By this Marchauntes tale it preveth weel.
>
> (R. 2421–5, H. 1209–13)

Chaucer, however, hopes that his readers will realise that it is the Merchant who tries to deceive us into accepting his warped views on women and marriage. January's extravagant praise of marriage belies the Merchant's heavy irony, and we know from *The General Prologue* that the latter is used to making pronouncements that sound profound and to concealing the truth. He lets his hero go through the same process of disillusionment of thinking marriage heaven, later fearing it might be purgatory, and finally finding it hell (see page 26). He makes January briefly contemplate then reject the anti-matrimonial sentiments which he himself must have held dear.

Yet the Merchant gives himself away by making January such an unattractive and lecherous character. His speeches reveal his hypocrisy and twisted thinking, for example when January says that there can be no lechery in marriage any more than a man can hurt himself with his own knife! The frequent references to money and possessions also tell us something about the Merchant's mercenary attitude to life.

Justinus and Pluto with their anti-feminist views would echo the Merchant's own feelings about women. Just as Pluto restored January's sight, thus opening his eyes to the true nature of his wife, so also does the Merchant wish to open the eyes of his hearers to the deceits of women. But the ultimate irony is that January is deceived once more by his wife, just as Chaucer wishes us to see that the Merchant, in spite of his fine rhetoric, is also deceived about women and marriage.

By the end of the tale, therefore, if we have not been convinced by the crafty Merchant or, like Harry Bailey, wish to think that all women are deceivers, we have learnt little about marriage but a lot about the Merchant. He appears an embittered and biased man who is aware of the socially, morally and theologically correct reasons for marrying, for instance to avoid lechery, to produce heirs, and so on, yet still makes generalisations about marriage based on the example of a senile man who simply wishes to possess a beautiful young girl.

None of the characters commands our respect: January's repulsive nature and appearance are immediately evident, May is a deceitful and bold-faced liar and Damian's concept of love seems to be rapid sexual satisfaction. Such unsympathetic characterisation also reflects the nature of the teller. There is, however, one problem that puzzles us. January is described in more disgusting terms than would surely suit the Merchant's purpose for his duped husband, his vision of the horrors of marriage is perhaps too exaggerated, and the rhetorical outbursts are so very evidently out of place in a fabliau. One solution might be that Chaucer's own controlling voice is at work here in case we are deluded, like Harry Bailey. Another possibility is that the Merchant's hypocrisy and bitterness, like the Pardoner's in another of the *Tales*, has blinded him to his listeners' natural reaction.

The Merchant therefore appears more like his self-deluded and blind hero, January, than he would wish us to think. Both are blind to reality, both hypocritically present a fine case in favour of marriage, yet their aims are suspect. The Merchant is blind to the Clerk's interpretation of marriage, and he tries to blind us by his abuse of logical debate and eloquence in a tale purporting to show that it is women who abuse eloquence to deceive their husbands. The Merchant is out of harmony with himself, like so many of Chaucer's characters, but the danger that he can sway us into believing his warped views on women and marriage is averted by Chaucer's own controlling voice, or, we might say, by the Merchant's error in thinking that his listeners also lack wisdom. As with all his tales Chaucer leaves the final answer to the individual reader and thus makes us question our own views on the topic.

The genre and style of *The Merchant's Tale*

The Merchant's Tale is usually grouped with the Miller's, Reeve's and Shipman's tales as a fabliau, yet it seems to defy categorisation as it contains elements of debate poetry and the sermon in addition. A fabliau (the word is connected with 'fable') is usually a low, humorous tale in verse and derives its name from twelfth- and thirteenth-century French stories of that nature. We have few true fabliaux preserved in English literature, probably because they were rarely written down, being passed on orally. Chaucer calls them *cherles tale[s]* that deal with *harlotrye*, that is, coarse characters' tales about crude events (see the *Miller's Tale* lines R. 3169ff.). The pear tree story would have been known from popular tales, although we have no precise source. The ingredients of such a fabliau are comic, crude events told in a dramatic way in verse, with lots of action which is vividly and visually described. If there is any moral at all, it concerns down-to-earth common-sense or rough revenge and justice. The characters are usually stereotypes, such as the old lover with the attractive young wife who is seduced by the handsome young man. There are no fine rhetorical passages and the language used is economical.

In Chaucer's fabliaux the young lovers sometimes parody the language of aristocratic courtly love in an attempt to ennoble their furtive and speedy escapades. Damian, for example, swoons, is love-sick and addresses May as is fitting for the courtly lover. May insists 'I am a gentil womman and no wenche' (R. 2202, H. 990), yet this façade of courtly talk is soon discarded when their basic instincts take over and talk is supplanted by action.

The story of January, May and Damian can be called a typical fabliau, expertly contrived by Chaucer to reveal the teller's crude nature and anti-feminist views. Yet, as we saw in *The General Prologue*, the teller is deceptive. He cloaks his base 'moral' in eloquent debate.

The initial part of the tale often strikes the reader as boring or at best out of place. It is a debate between those in favour of marriage, January and Placebo, backed up by Christian teaching, and those against it, Justinus and contemporary anti-matrimonial teaching. January in this section is not a typical fabliau husband, like John the Carpenter in *The Miller's Tale*. He is a subtle debater who skilfully hides his lustful desire to possess a young girl in marriage by sanctimonious sermonising on the spiritual reasons for marriage. The fine rhetoric he uses and the time spent on discussion are all unnecessary, as January has made up his mind from the beginning. The common-sense and anti-matrimonial arguments that the Merchant himself probably shared fall on deaf ears, while Placebo the flatterer's arguments do no more than echo January's, no matter what January would have said.

Why, then, this apparently unnecessary superstructure of a well-formed medieval debate, correct in all its parts, yet morally misplaced? We get the impression of the Merchant as a subtle debater, as is also suggested in *The General Prologue* – that is, someone who has the gift of eloquence. Chaucer, therefore, can only be interested in demonstrating the dangers of the abuse of eloquence by inserting this long discussion which contributes nothing to the basic story. It is highly ironical that the Merchant should state that not even Marcian, the poet Martianus Capella, who wrote about 'the Wedding of Philology and Mercury', had the rhetorical power to describe the magnificent marriage of January and May (R. 1732–7, H. 520–5). This work is about the joining of Philology or Eloquence with Mercury or Wisdom. The implications of this theme are discussed on pages 53–5, but the point that Chaucer makes is that eloquent expression should convey wise thoughts and not be abused by deluding people into believing wrong ideas. January is far from being the personification of Wisdom, and May uses the gift of eloquence for deceitful purposes.

Just as the Merchant attempts to beguile us by the initial display of rhetoric, so also during the narration of the fabliau he interposes passages in a lofty style which seem out of place and slow up the otherwise swiftly moving narration. There is, for example, the pompous exclamation concerning Fortune ('O sodeyn hap! o . . . Fortune unstable! . . .' R. 2057ff., H. 845ff.) The passage is an outraged diatribe on Fortune's instability, a popular sentiment in the Middle Ages; but man was encouraged to overcome the blows of worldly fortune by trusting in divine providence. The emotional outburst shows the importance January and the narrator give to physical sight to the exclusion of inner enlightenment. A similarly melodramatic exclamation (the rhetorical device is called *exclamatio*) occurs when the narrator berates unfaithful servants: 'O perilous fyr . . . ' (R. 1783–94, H. 571–82). Both passages contain needless repetitions and ironies, for example when Damian is compared to 'the naddre in bosom sly untrewe', 'the sly, unfaithful adder in the breast'!

At the other extreme we find passages of swift narrative:

He stoupeth doun, and on his bak she stood,
And caughte hire by a twiste and up she gooth.

(R. 2348–9, H. 1136–7)

The poetry itself reflects the quick, breathless action with its 'and—and—and' clauses and monosyllabic words. In the fabliau section the direct speech is also lively and colloquial:

'Strugle!' quod he, 'ye algate in it wente!
God yeve yow bothe on shames deth to dyen!'

(R. 2376–7, H. 1164–5)

January, like the Wife of Bath, enjoys preaching and quoting—or rather misquoting—texts and proverbs. He addresses his wife in the lyrical tones of the Song of Solomon in lines R. 2138–48, H. 926–36, yet completely misses the symbolic implications of what he has said (see page 35). The difference between perfect marriage and his furtive dashes into the garden is thereby underlined. His proverbs also rebound on himself, for example, when he says

'Bet is,' quod he, 'a pyk than a pykerel,
And bet than old boef is the tendre veel'

(R. 1419–20, H. 207–8)

His choice of imagery reflects his animalistic attitude towards women and shows his selfishness, especially as he is no young chicken himself. The visual image we do have of him, on the contrary, is far from that of the virile lover. Echoing January's own choice of animalistic images, the poet slyly evokes comparisons with an old fowl:

And ful of jargon as a flekked pye [magpie].
The slakke skyn aboute his nekke shaketh,
Whil that he sang, so chaunteth he and craketh.
(R. 1848–51, H. 636–8)

The tale is full of visual and auditory delights, as, for example, in the above quotation with the 'slakke skyn' alliteration. Or take the example of May's cold fear in the line 'The bryde was broght abedde as stille as stoon', with its double alliteration. We should *listen* to the tale as the early audience did, rather than *read* it, for much of the meaning is reinforced by the sound. Surely the most evocative passage must be the wedding night scene, when, after all the lofty sermonising and romantic talk we see the grim reality. Such poetry with its visual and tactile associations shows the unparalleled art of Chaucer:

He lulleth hire, he kisseth hire ful ofte;
With thikke brustles of his berd unsofte,
Lyk to the skyn of houndfyssh, sharp as brere—
For he was shave al newe in his manere—
He rubbeth hire aboute hir tendre face.

(R. 1823–7, H. 611–15)

The link between *The Clerk's Tale* and *The Merchant's Tale*

Chaucer sometimes guides our opinion of a pilgrim by the way he or she interprets the preceding tale. We have seen how Harry Bailey's ready agreement with the Merchant about women and marriage reflects his own experience and character. Similarly the message which the Merchant gleans from the preceding tale by the Clerk tells us much about him. The first line of the Merchant's *Prologue*, 'Wepyng and waylyng, care and oother sorwe,' echoes the final line of *The Clerk's Tale*: 'And lat hym care, and wepe, and wrynge, and waille!' ('Let him [the husband] be troubled, weep, squirm and cry'). The Clerk had told a moral tale about the obedient Griselda who was constantly tested by her husband, Walter. The moral is that everyone should be 'constant in adversitee', that is, strong in times of trouble, thereby showing one's faith. He concludes by implying that God tests mankind, as Walter tested his wife, in order to strengthen faith and aid spiritual growth.

The Wife of Bath had earlier 'preached' to women about how they should dominate their husbands and use marriage for their own financial gain. She therefore begins a debate on marriage that the Clerk, Merchant and Franklin pick up. To a certain extent the tale of the obedient wife Griselda is a reply to the Wife of Bath's abuse of the sacrament of marriage, but the Clerk intends us to see the broader implications for humanity in the need to overcome adversity by having strong faith. At the very end of his tale the Clerk adds an amusing passage in order to conclude on a lighter note, but it is also a jibe at the Wife of Bath. This passage might be summed up as follows: 'Now, good wives, do not let a priest like me tell you to be humble like Griselda. Do not obey your husbands, have a sharp tongue in your head, pierce him with your bitter eloquence, make him jealous and make him suffer!' Naturally the Clerk is not serious when he says this, as his tale implies the opposite, but the Merchant, still smarting from his own marital experiences, catches on to this frivolous conclusion.

For this reason there are many deliberate similarities and contrasts when we compare the two tales: both Walter and January are wealthy and influential men from Lombardy who choose girls of lower social status as wives, and neither considers for a moment the possibility that his offer would be refused. The similarities then end, as the Merchant wishes to show that, in reality, wives differ greatly from patient Griselda:

Ther is a long and large difference
Bitwixt Griseldis grete pacience
And of my wyf the passyng crueltee

(R. 1223–5, H. 11–13)

He therefore makes his naïve January believe that all wives are Griseldas: 'For who kan be so buxom [obedient] as a wyf?' (R. 1287, H. 75), although his aims are vastly different from Walter's.

It therefore helps our understanding of the Merchant and his tale to look at them in the context of *The Canterbury Tales* as a whole and to study the preceding tale by the Clerk in particular. The Wife of Bath tells women how to make the most of unequal matches; the Merchant wishes to show us what it is like to be a deceived husband, yet in fact tells us more about the shaky foundations he builds his marriage on; while the Clerk presents us with the dry, theoretical view of marriage held by the Church. None of them presents the key to the perfect marriage, and the problem is never solved in *The Canterbury Tales*, not even in *The Franklin's Tale* in which equality in marriage is suggested. As ever, Chaucer raises vital issues and presents various views as objectively as possible, without giving solutions. But what is clearly evident is the dichotomy in the Middle Ages between theory and practice: the message taught by the Church concerning marriage and what society demanded.

Some major themes

The theme of the garden

The theme of the garden in medieval literature is steeped in symbolism. The garden provides the setting for many romances, especially those in the courtly love tradition. The lovers in *The Knight's Tale* and Dorigen and Aurelius in *The Franklin's Tale*, for example, meet in walled gardens of great beauty. Much of the inspiration for this setting comes from the handbook of courtly love, the thirteenth-century French poem *Le Roman de la Rose*, which Chaucer translated, calling it *The Romaunt of the Rose*. Only true lovers, those hit by Cupid's dart, can enter this walled garden of love, and the Merchant tells us (R. 2031–3, H. 819–21) that January's garden of pleasure even surpassed the description of that in *Le Roman de la Rose*.

The second thing we learn about the garden is that January sees it as his very own possession: 'He made a gardyn . . . ' and 'he wol no wight suffren bere the keye/Save he hymself . . . '. He owns the garden as he thinks he owns May, as his private property, and we are continually reminded of the key to that garden and thereby May's love, both of which he thinks he alone owns. Both the garden and May are fresh, beautiful, fertile—and potentially dangerous; they are objects of pleasure for the old, lecherous knight, and they both prove to be his downfall. There are also parallels here with the garden whence Pluto abducted Proserpina in the myth, and the scene of natural fertility provides an ironic background for the 'games' January devises in the garden: 'And thynges whiche that were nat doon abedde,/He in the gardyn parfourned hem and spedde' (R. 2051–2, H. 839–40).

By suggesting that there had never existed a fairer garden (R. 2030, H. 818) associations of Eden and paradise are conjured up. January calls May 'his paradys', and, as mentioned above, there are many similarities between garden and wife. Both Eden and this garden had a snake in them which led to a moral downfall, the snake in the tree being in the shape of Damian in this tale. In medieval times it was not only the apple that was considered to be the fruit of the tree in the Garden of Eden (Genesis 3), and we are surely meant to see the similarity between the Fall of Man, brought about by Eve, and May's request to climb into the tree to reach the 'fruit' that she desires.

We might even pursue the possible symbolism of the tree in the garden further. It was accepted in the Middle Ages that the cross of Christ was made of the same wood as the tree in Eden. Christ was called the second Adam, he who undid the first Adam's sin by not yielding to temptation. In illustrations of the Crucifixion in the Middle Ages we often find the snake and the skull of Adam included. The final scene of Damian and May in the tree is made all the more ridiculous and ironic if we consider the significance of the Crucifixion, for in the tale we have a young man, Damian, named after the patron saint of healing, 'struggling' on a tree supposedly in order to heal January of his blindness, while for him the supposed 'salvation' of January is an excuse for adultery.

The irony is heightened by January's allusions to himself as a blossoming tree. He says that although he is white-haired he might be compared to a tree in blossom, which is a sign that fruit will come later, 'And blosmy tree nys neither drye ne deed' (R. 1463, H. 251). His heart and his limbs are as green as a laurel tree, he concludes, and the laurel tree is also mentioned as appearing in his garden (R. 2037, H. 825), beside the well that reminds one of the well of Narcissus in *Le Roman de la Rose*, and January's love is indeed self-centred.

The Reeve in *The Canterbury Tales* in a similar way compares himself to a leek. Although I have white hair, he says, I have a green tail, and although 'oure myghte be goon,/Oure wyl desireth folie evere in oon'; that is, although he is no longer virile he still seeks folly. The Merchant graphically paints the scene of January's wedding night, and we would agree with the Reeve that it shows more folly than virility, in spite of the picture January tries to give of himself as a great lover. The fertile nature of the garden, therefore, provides an amusing and ironic backcloth for the foolish antics of the old lover. It is here that January performs things he cannot do abed and where, on holiday from their infertile world, Pluto and Proserpina quarrel. All are equally unproductive and blind but, unlike Adam and Eve, they leave this potential paradise, unaware of their folly and flaws. No lesson is learned, except perhaps by Chaucer's readers.

January's erotic expectations in the garden are stressed by the reference to Priapus, the god both of gardens and male eroticism (R. 2034, H. 822). January's Garden of Paradise, like his marriage, does indeed turn into a hell, inhabited significantly by the King and Queen of the Underworld.

The garden, then, initially conjures up images of delight, fertility and romance, but, like all worldly things in the tale, including love and marriage, all depends on the use made of it. The characters are deceitful, lustful and sexually violent, thereby excluding themselves from what could have been a paradise. A final touch of irony occurs in the garden when May begs Mary 'that is of hevene queene' (R. 2334, H. 1122) to help her in her plight. The Virgin Mary, also known as the second Eve as she undid the sins of Eve in Eden, is hardly likely to rush to the aid of someone trying to commit adultery. It is therefore fitting that it is the Queen of the Underworld who comes to May's rescue in the end.

The themes of love and marriage

It is necessary to differentiate between these two themes in the Middle Ages, as marriage and reciprocal love rarely seemed to go together, at least not in the merchant and noble classes. Marriage was very much a business deal for political reasons amongst the aristocracy and a matter of economics with the bourgeoisie. The Wife of Bath admirably shows how marriage can be used to gain wealth and social position, and, as in *The Merchant's Tale*, there is usually much talk about dowries and financial contracts surrounding weddings. The Merchant states that it would take too long if he told us about every writ and bond by which May was endowed with January's land or about all the fine array she received (R. 1696–9, H. 484–7).

May's motives are significantly unknown, as her role is a passive one. Perhaps, like Proserpina, she had no choice, or, like the Wife of Bath, she saw a chance to advance herself socially and economically. Whatever her reasons, it was a marriage totally devoid of reciprocal love. Her initial passivity parallels the obedience of Griselda, and neither Walter in *The Clerk's Tale* nor January contemplates for a second the thought that the girl might refuse his munificent offer. May is discussed in the passive voice even: 'She . . . Shal wedded be unto this Januarie' (R. 1695, H. 483). She sits silently, looking gracious and beautiful throughout the feast, simply an object of beauty possessed by a rich man. Even her thoughts are hidden: 'God woot [knows] what that May thoughte in hir herte' (R. 1851, H. 639).

The old knight's reasons for marriage are quite obvious. In spite of all his fine talk about propagation and religious reasons, it is evident that his criteria are purely sexual: his wife must be young and beautiful:

> Many fair shap and many a fair visage
> Ther passeth thurgh his herte nyght by nyght,
> As whoso tooke a mirour polisshed bryght,
> And sette it in a commune market-place.
>
> (R. 1580–3, H. 368–71)

This curious image tells us a lot. The knight views women in his dreams as one who sees the reflection of one woman after the other pass over a mirror he holds up in the market-place. By this we see that it is the silent and passive *appearance* that is his only standard, and, secondly, the fact that the mirror is in the market-place stresses the commercial, business deal he imagines marriage to be. He has money and she has sexual attraction which he can buy. What he gets is indeed a young and beautiful woman, but he does not count on her having her own feelings and needs.

The Wife of Bath in her tale gives a knight the choice in marriage between an unattractive but virtuous old hag or a beautiful but unfaithful young girl. The traditional conclusion to this tale is that after he has wisely chosen the old hag, she becomes beautiful as well. Naturally the Wife of Bath twists this story to promote her own theme of female mastery in marriage, but in terms of this well-known folk-tale January makes the wrong decision and has to reap the consequences.

The Church condoned such an unequal marriage: the priest blessed them, said the usual prayers and make all 'siker ynogh with hoolinesse' (R. 1708, H. 496), and later blessed the marital bed. The endorsement of this match by the Church and the glamour of the sumptuous wedding feast which is hyperbolically described conceal the grim reality of the event, but Chaucer graphically depicts the horror of the wedding night in all its sordid details. This vivid contrast highlights the double morality concerning marriage in the Middle Ages. Church and society gloss over and indeed applaud what can be a grotesque existence. The Wife of Bath found a solution and played the game society wished her to, but she made the very best of the situation financially.

Young women trapped in such a marriage were practically forced into adultery, as were men who were obliged to marry for political or economic reasons (for instance, Jankyn in *The Wife of Bath's Prologue*). May also finds a solution by achieving sexual fulfilment with Damian while enjoying the higher social position and wealth bestowed on her by marriage.

Courtly love

Mutual or romantic love does however exist in medieval literature and the first rule is that it cannot happen in marriage, according to the so-called code of courtly love or *fin amour* outlined in Andreas Capellanus's *The Art of Courtly Love*. The lover has to be young, ardent, humble, obedient to his lady, courteous to all and noble in mind. He is expected to faint and become ill because of his great love, and to exchange letters with his lady. The mistress has to be initially aloof, to dominate in the affair and finally to show pity. Above all the affair must be kept secret. Such behaviour can be found in many of Chaucer's works, such as *Troilus and Criseyde* and *The Knight's Tale*; indeed it forms the basic code in all courtly romances. Glamour, escapism and romance are achieved by dressing up an illicit love affair as an elaborate, courtly game. A religion of love, which in many respects parallels the cult of the Virgin Mary, covers over the fact that sin is committed. It is difficult to say whether such behaviour was actually practised or whether it was a literary phenomenon.

In *The Miller's Tale* and *The Merchant's Tale* there is a parody of such courtly behaviour amongst the young lovers. It would appear as if they soften the reality of adultery by pretending to be romantic figures. Damian pines away for the love of his lady and becomes ill, they exchange letters, keep the affair secret, and so on. But May is all too eager to accept her young lover and is not at all aloof. Such a ready submission by the lady is not in keeping with the rules of courtly love, so the narrator, probably with tongue in cheek, claims that May is thus expressing the noble virtue of 'pitee', a word which is repeated three times (R. 1979, H. 767; R. 1986, H. 774; R. 1995, H. 783). The romantic embellishment is quickly forgotten in both fabliaux, however, as the characters get down to business. May shoves the love letter down the toilet and goes about the practical business of forging keys and making a rendezvous, while the final scene of crude fumbling in a tree can hardly be called courtly at all.

It would appear as if Chaucer condones neither alliance. Youth and Age will never make a good match, yet adultery cannot provide the solution, no matter how romantically it is presented.

The Church's views on marriage

Marriage in the later Middle Ages was a holy sacrament, that is, a religious rite that symbolises something spiritual and usually involves a pledge, as, for instance, in baptism and penance. In addition the sacrament of marriage defined one's social status and sanctioned the Church's authority. In the fourteenth century girls were often married when twelve to fourteen and boys at fourteen to sixteen, and there are examples of very much younger children being married. Symkyn's daughter in *The Reeve's Tale* is practically an old maid, being unmarried at twenty.

Stress was laid on the symbolic significance of marriage at the ceremony. The bride would represent Ecclesia, the Church, (and in some countries wear a crown), and the groom symbolised Christ. The Parson in *The Canterbury Tales* clearly states that marriage signifies the knitting together of Christ and of Holy Church, and that, as the Church on earth submits to Christ, so also must the wife be ruled by her husband. Then both promised to love each other. The passage from the Bible, Ephesians 5:23, was frequently quoted in this context: 'For the husband is the head of the wife, even as Christ is the head of the Church.' Marriage symbolised the coming together of spiritual and worldly elements: reason and passion, soul and body, heaven and earth.

Although virginity and widowhood were considered superior to marriage, marriage was not sinful in any way, only less perfect than virginity, as Christ was celibate. But January makes a fatal mistake which would have been quickly noticed by the medieval audience. He has been a lecherous bachelor until the opening of the tale, when he thinks that he had better settle down to marry, as he fears for his soul. Yet he chooses a wife for lecherous reasons and wrongly thinks that one cannot commit a sin with one's wife. He claims that he knows the Church's reasons for permitting marriage, namely to avoid lechery and to have children and to aid one another, but, he mischievously adds, that is not for him. Marriage for him is an insurance policy which will permit him to continue his lecherous activities and, he thinks, still go to heaven. But in this he is as much mistaken as when he says that a man cannot harm himself with his own knife (R. 1839–41, H. 627–9). Chaucer's Parson comments on such conduct under the heading of Lechery. Here is a translation of it:

> 'The third type of adultery is between a man and his wife and that is when they pay no proper consideration to their union, but only to their fleshly delight . . . they think that because they are married everything is good enough. But the devil controls such people'
>
> (*The Parson's Tale*, R. 900–5, translated).

The theme of Eloquence and Wisdom

We saw in the section above how marriage in the Middle Ages symbolised the unification of all things worldly with those spiritual. Worldly gifts, such as love, marriage, the power of eloquence and so on, are not in themselves bad or good, but all depends on whether or not they are 'married' to the spirit. Just as reason should control passion, so also should wisdom control what we say—that is, our power of eloquence. In brief, fine speech should convey fine thoughts, and it was an abuse of God's gift of eloquence to do otherwise. This is a major theme in many of the tales, as some pilgrims try to convince us of their morally flawed views in persuasive, flawless rhetoric. The Wife of Bath is an expert in arguing, using partially quoted texts and dubious proverbs; the Clerk comments on the dangers of 'crabbed bitter eloquence', a theme which the Parson takes up in a section where he lists all abuses of speech, such as lies and flattery (*Parson's Tale*, R. 600–50). The Merchant tries to convince us that women's deceiving rhetoric is the source of marital trouble, the Squire manages to say very little in exaggerated and prolonged rhetorical passages, and the Franklin, in spite of his self-effacing plea 'I lerned nevere rhetorik', presents a rhetorically perfect tale but with a suspect moral. In short, it was a theme that fascinated Chaucer.

The first part of *The Merchant's Tale* comprises a long rhetorical debate about marriage. Different viewpoints are solicited, opinions are contrasted and weighed, but to no avail so far as January is concerned. He has made up his mind before the tale begins and the only person he will listen to is the flatterer Placebo. The Parson states, however, concerning flattery:

> 'Let us now touch on the vice of flattery, which does not come willingly but from fear or covetousness. Flattery is usually wrongful praising. Flattery is the devil's nurse, that nourishes his children with the milk of flattery . . . . Flatterers are the devil's chaplains that forever sing *Placebo* ["I shall please"].'
>
> (*The Parson's Tale*, R. 612–15, translated)

The Merchant's Placebo simply reflects January's own views uncritically. This long section, therefore, serves the purpose of showing us how January is able to twist authorities, how he is deaf to all reasonable arguments and how he can rationalise in fine rhetoric his base desire to possess a young girl. He goes through the correct 'channels', namely, he asks for wisdom from his friends, but it is the 'flesh' or animal instincts that finally makes the decision, not the 'head' or wisdom.

It is not surprising, therefore, that the tale the Merchant tells is basically a crude fabliau and not a moral sermon. His attempts to embellish this low tale all appear ridiculous. January at the beginning poses as the wise debater and it is ironical that his wife should turn out to be equally eloquent. It is not by chance that Chaucer slips in a reference to the fifth-century Carthaginian author Martianus Cappela's *The Marriage of Philology and Mercury*. Not even the great rhetorician Marcian, the Merchant states, would have the ability to describe the splendours of the magnificent wedding between January and May. Mercury is the god of wisdom (and also the Roman god of commerce, which adds further irony), and Philology implies language or the gift of speech. The Merchant, therefore, is debasing his gift of eloquence to elevate the wedding to such ridiculous heights, even though he is being satirical, and the unlikely comparison between the perfect 'marriage' of wisdom and eloquence with that of the Lombardian couple highlights their incompatibility and folly.

Every character in the tale, including the narrator, is guilty of this vice. Justinus and Pluto eloquently argue against the sacrament of marriage; Proserpina and May abuse eloquence for deceitful and immoral purposes; Placebo flatters; Damian dresses up his lust in language of courtly romance, while January covers his selfish desires in the rhetoric of scholarly debate.

The Merchant himself might be said to be the major abuser of eloquence. He hears the wisdom of the Clerk's tale, blinds himself to the spiritual implications, because of his own warped values, and then tells a brilliant tale that attempts to convince us that all women are deceivers and all marriages are hell. But as always Chaucer plants enough clues along the way to open our eyes to the illogical conclusions the characters come to, and thus makes his major theme the dangers of the abuse of eloquence.

The Pluto and Proserpina theme

At first it might appear that the episode with Pluto and Proserpina in the garden was an unnecessary intrusion or simply added as a device to bring about the restoration of January's sight. Chaucer never seems to add extraneous material, and apparent irrelevancies as far as plot is concerned invariably reflect the character of the teller.

A minor function of this episode is to create dramatic suspense at the climax of the fabliau by tantalisingly forcing us to wait before we can witness the inevitable catastrophe. More significant, however, is the way that the characters of Pluto and Proserpina aptly parallel January and May, and by comparing the two sets of characters the shortcomings of the hero and heroine are highlighted. Chaucer gave his two major characters symbolic names: January and May. January implies the depth of cold winter, old age and infertility. He forces himself on the young and tender May in a harsh and violent fashion, is jealous and is determined to dominate.

Pluto, according to the legend by Claudian which Chaucer states is his source (R. 2232, H. 1020), lives in the underworld, Hades, and is in constant darkness like the blind January. Pluto has two brothers, Jove and Neptune, who help him to find a wife, whom Pluto forcibly abducts with the help of Venus, the goddess of love. This is all we know from the Claudian source, but the myth of Pluto and Proserpina traditionally continues with the story of how she escaped from Pluto on condition that she would spend one third of the year with him in Hades as Queen of the Underworld and the rest of the year with Ceres (Demeter in Greek mythology), her mother, who was the goddess of fertility. The myth explains why the land is barren part of the year and fruitful the rest of the time. Pluto's name implies 'wealth', which makes another parallel with the rich old knight. Pluto, therefore, is associated with old age, riches, blindness, winter, barrenness, rape and domination, while Proserpina conjures up images of fertility, the female spirit, spring and also clever (or deceitful) escape from her hell. Their marriage is the unification of opposites: what is bliss for Pluto is hell for Proserpina, and hell or Hades is the location of their married lives.

The parallels are obvious: May brings a breath of spring into January's winter, she is pregnant (or pretends to be) and deceitful in her escape; she delights in the fruitful garden of love and symbolically finds her bliss in a fruit tree.

The sterility, blindness and negative effect of selfish male domination are underlined by the inclusion of this episode. By placing both pairs in a garden, reminiscent of Eden and a heaven on earth, the difference between mutual love and selfish lust is emphasised. Venus aids both men, but it is the dangerous Venus of fire and passion that laughs at January's marriage (R. 1723, H. 512) and causes Damian to faint, 'so soore hath Venus hurt hym with hire brond' (R. 1777, H. 565). It is the same Venus that the Wife of Bath claims has influenced her.

The gifts that the mythological pair gave their human counterparts are also significant. From Pluto January receives physical sight but not inner illumination—that is, wisdom or even common sense, and the gift is worthless as it simply complicates the issue. No change occurs either in Pluto's attitude to women or January's view of marriage. Similarly Proserpina's gift to May, of a subtle tongue to lie her way out of the situation, is also far from praiseworthy. Indeed May appears to be good at quick thinking and clever talk already, as we can see in her speech in lines R. 2188–206, H. 976–94 and R. 2329–37, H. 1117–25. The gift is that which the lecherous Wife of Bath possesses, namely the abuse of eloquence, a 'gift' which the Merchant himself demonstrates. The theme of the abuse of rhetoric or eloquence matters greatly in the tale, and Pluto's fine speech on the deceits of women and the counter-argument by Proserpina help to substantiate Chaucer's aim. Proserpina's gift is significantly the power of speech to deceive, while Pluto's gift is the power of vision without wisdom.

The major characters

January

Just as the tale is a mixture of fabliau and debate, so also is January both a comic character and an eloquent disputer. Firstly he appears as the stock figure of the *senex amans*, the old lover, who becomes the cuckolded husband in many fabliaux. The audience would have recognised this figure immediately and remembered the many warnings, such as that at the beginning of *The Miller's Tale*, that youth and age do not go well together in marriage:

> Men sholde wedden after hire estaat,
> For youthe and elde [old age] is often at debaat.
>
> (R. 3229–30)

However, January states to the contrary that

> it is a glorious thyng,
> And namely whan a man is oold and hoor;
> Thanne is a wyf the fruyt of his tresor.
> Thanne sholde he take a yong wyf and a feir,
> On which he myghte engendren hym an heir.
>
> (R. 1268–72, H. 56–60)

Placebo, the flatterer, echoes this sentiment, saying 'it is an heigh corage/Of any man that stapen is in age/To take a yong wyf' (R. 1513–15, H. 301–3). Justinus, however, warns him about the dangers of marrying a young girl, as even a young man would need all his time to satisfy her (R. 1559–61, H. 343–5).

Apart from his foolish plan to marry a lively young girl, January also appears ridiculous by his naïve statements about marriage, many of which prove to be ironic—that is, they convey more to us than January intends because of our superior knowledge of the events. An example of this dramatic irony occurs in the above quotation (R. 1270, H. 58) in which a wife is called the fruit of the husband's treasure. We immediately think of the fruit in January's garden that brought about his downfall, and also of the fruit in Eden that broke up the perfect marriage. January's allusion to himself as a tree in blossom about to bear fruit (R. 1461–6, H. 249–54) is similarly ironic. He states that far too many people speak about marriage who know as much about the subject as his own servant (R. 1442–5, H. 230–3); as Damian is his servant, we know that *his* servant at least knows more about wives' needs than does his master. January wishes for a young wife, because she will therefore be obedient and as pliable as warm wax (R. 1430, H. 218), but the comparison is ironic, as we know that May will not only be disobedient but also use warm wax to deceive her husband. A constant source of irony is to be found in January's repeated references to marriage as a paradise, when in fact we see his paradisial garden later turned into a hell—at least for the cuckolded husband. Such ironies abound in the tale and most come from January, thus making him appear more naïve and ridiculous.

The Merchant presents us with a hero who is sixty (very old in the Middle Ages), unmarried but by no means celibate, a 'worthy', rich knight living in the banking centre of Lombardy and a senile fool who is blind to the realities of women's deceits. This is how the Merchant, the bankrupt pilgrim who still smarts from his miserable, two-month-old marriage, wishes us to see January. He deliberately creates a hero of similar social status, wealth and geographic origins as the Clerk's Walter, in order to show the vast difference between what the Clerk presents as the perfect wife and what he (the Merchant) knows is the reality of marriage. He wishes to make the gap between theory and practice as wide as possible, so he also makes his hero an eloquent debater who is well aware of the contemporary arguments in favour of and against marriage. Marriage helps one to avoid lust, to have children, and to aid one another, January states, echoing medieval Christian teaching, yet his hypocrisy is seen by his constant insistence that the wife of his choice must be a sexual object, irrespective of her morality. His most 'religious' thought is that he will escape hell-fire by marrying, but this simply reflects his flawed thinking.

The Merchant allows his debater to consider the contemporary anti-matrimonial views which Pluto later repeats, and which he himself must have supported. January paraphrases the arguments in Theophrastus's *The Golden Book of Marriage*, a well-known anti-matrimonial work that is mentioned in *The Wife of Bath's Prologue* (R. 671), yet he finally rejects them with an authoritative 'Deffie Theofraste, and herke me' (R. 1310, H. 98).

The Merchant's cynical aim, however, is evident in the way he makes his hero's praise of marriage hyperbolic and artificial; every man should kneel all his life in thanks to God for his wife, he dramatically exclaims (R. 1350−2, H. 138−40). January also undercuts his own arguments by quoting shaky examples and suspect proverbs to back up his argument. As can be seen from the Notes and Glossaries, the examples of Rebecca, Judith, Abigail and Esther as perfect wives are hardly the most fitting; rather they would better fit Pluto's list of dangerous women.

With similar impropriety and exaggeration January addresses May when they are about to enter their paradisial garden with a parody of the beautiful poetry from the biblical Song of Solomon:

'Rys up, my wyf, my love, my lady free!
The turtles voys is herd, my dowve sweete;
The wynter is goon with alle his reynes weete.
Com forth now, with thyne eyen columbyn!'
(R. 2138−41, H. 926−9)

In the Middle Ages this beautiful passage was interpreted as Christ's words to the Church who represents the New Law of charity. The old, corrupt law of winter (January?) has passed and Christian love has entered the world. This biblical text has been said to express the highest love that could be conceived, yet January calls the passage 'olde lewed words' (R. 2149, H. 937), 'lewed' implying ignorant or coarse. Any crude interpretation can only be in January's mind; he is not mocking the biblical text, but his reading it as a lewd invitation to erotic love reflects his own blindness to any higher love than sexual. The dual significance of the word 'lewed' as both lustful and ignorant ideally sums up January's approach to marriage.

For January, love and marriage imply not only eroticism but also economic investment. The expression quoted above, 'a wyf is the fruyt of his tresor' suggests, apart from the irony, that she is the type of product that a rich old man can afford. The market-place image (R. 1580 ff., H. 368 ff.) substantiates this attitude of buying the *image* of a beautiful, silent, obedient woman. Robert Browning's (1812–89) poem 'My Last Duchess', in which the Count is seen to prefer his wives as portraits in a gallery rather than as live beings, expresses much the same sentiment. We assume that January bought May at a high price, when we consider the number of endowments she received (R. 1696 ff., H. 484 ff.). Just as a miser jealously locks his treasure in a chest, so January keeps May in a walled garden to which he alone has the key. Even in religious terms he sees her as an insurance policy against eternal damnation. January is not criticised by the teller for viewing marriage in this way, and we are left to believe that the Merchant, whose world is also that of commerce, reflects his own opinion that wives are not the economic investment they ought to be and that gold and servants are preferable.

January is a very complex character: at times a fabliau fool, at times a debater who shows his knowledge of the Bible, classics, Church Fathers and proverbs, yet is invariably blind to the texts' true interpretation. At the beginning we laugh at his naïvety, question his abuse of textual sources and eloquence, and scorn his hypocritical camouflaging of lust in fine language. After the marriage our laughter at his self-delusion turns to contempt and disgust as we see how he treats May, abusing his wealth to possess a young girl. Then finally we feel pity for him as he pathetically tries to hold on to his possession and is hopelessly duped. Such complexity does not reflect confused thinking by Chaucer, rather his genius at changing a stock, one-dimensional fabliau figure into a credible, multi-faceted human-being with all his imperfections, follies, tragedy, pathos, humour and joy.

May

May, like many of the fabliaux wives, is a beautiful, young, tender girl who sparks off amorous thoughts in all the men around her. She is a catalyst, a pretty girl who causes men to react and thus the plot to unfold. May is of a lower social class than her husband, poorer and much younger, the typical fabliau wife caught in an unequal marriage of youth and age. This is a common theme in medieval literature, for instance, in *The Miller's Tale* where the Miller warns that 'men should marry a woman similar to themselves, for youth and old age are often in disagreement.'

At the beginning May is seen and not heard; in fact just what January wishes, as we realise from the 'mirror in the market-place' image (see page 50). She is the passive object of his lust, whose actions are described in the passive voice (R. 1695, H. 483). He thinks that she will be as pliable as 'warm wax' (R. 1430, H. 218), namely an obedient plaything who will allow him to continue his licentious life but with the blessing of the Church and therefore assured entry into heaven. Later, of course, we are to see the use she makes of warm wax to deceive January. She is told to be faithful by the priest who blesses this unequal match, and she silently sits throughout the feast looking gracious and radiant. We hear in detail about January's thoughts and preparations on the wedding night, while May, the object of his desires, is 'broght abedde as stille as stoon'. The image confirms the passivity and adds the feeling of coldness and even fear on her part. The camera is focused on January throughout the wedding night and his words and actions create the horrific and pathetic picture of an old man's attempt to be a great lover. May is again silent, but the author with great understatement adds 'But God woot [knows] what that May thoughte in hir herte' (R. 1851, H. 639). January is the 'werkman' in this scene, yet it is May who is obliged by tradition to remain in her room for four days, 'For every labour somtyme moot han reste' (R. 1862, H. 650). In this section of the tale, therefore, May is only seen in connection with January: she is 'his fressh May, his paradys, his make [mate]'.

January naïvely sends her to Damian in order to comfort him, and she then becomes the object of Damian's advances. But the tables are turned in this relationship, because now she is the richer and socially superior partner. She becomes the instigator of the plot and the one who tells Damian what to do. We hear her own thoughts in lines R. 1982–5, H. 770–3 when she makes up her mind to love Damian. This uncourtly and adulterous intention is quickly excused by the narrator—probably sarcastically as we know the Merchant's anti-feminist feelings—by saying that she yields out of pity: 'Lo, pitee renneth soone in gentil herte' (R. 1986, H. 774). If 'gentil' implies noble, then it was well known that the noble lady did not yield to her lover immediately, and if 'gentil' refers to nobility of spirit, then her intended adultery would hardly be in keeping. It is evident that she is led by physical desire and we now see a very different May. All the verbs are now active—*she* wrote a letter which *she* places under his pillow, *she* granted him her favour, *she* signals to Damian when January cannot see, *she* makes the impression of the key, and *she* tells Damian to climb the tree.

> For verraily he knew al hire entente,
> And every signe that she koude make,
> Wel bet than Januarie, hir owene make;
> For in a lettre she hadde toold hym al
> Of this matere, how he werchen shal.

(R. 2212–16, H. 1000–4)

Damian, after the initial proposal, plays less and less of an active role, while May directs the plot. We might even question the fact that Proserpina's gift to May is so magical, as she appears sufficiently quick-witted and eloquently persuasive before receiving it, to extricate herself from her predicament.

Whether or not May is really pregnant, we do not know, but it is necessary for her plot to convince January that she is in that state and therefore has an unusually strong craving for a pear. She asks for help, invoking the Virgin Mary, and the irony in her choice of patron is obvious. She very cleverly thinks of all contingencies, and forestalls January's fear of her infidelity when she is out of his reach by telling him to put his arms around the tree to prevent anyone climbing up to her: 'For wel I woot that ye mystruste me'. Then she stands on top of her husband, demonstrating symbolically that now she has the dominant position in their marriage.

May proves to be one of the those 'archwives' that the Clerk had mentioned at the conclusion of his tale, and very like the Wife of Bath, who also had the gift of chiding, accusing and deceiving. The Merchant therefore agrees with the Wife that *all* women are eloquent deceivers who master their husbands, have lovers and make marriage hell. But Chaucer has made May in the second half of the tale sufficiently unattractive to lose the sympathy she gained earlier. Marriage, Chaucer implies, is the hell or the heaven you make of it. The major difference between *The Wife of Bath's Prologue* and this tale is that January remains blind to his wife's deceit; he kisses her and strokes her as they return to his palace. May, it would appear, has managed to gain the best of both worlds.

Damian

Damian is more of a stereotype than January and May. He is the inevitable third member of the love triangle consisting of old husband, young wife and young lover. He is like Aurelius in *The Franklin's Tale* or Nicholas in *The Miller's Tale*, a lusty bachelor who adds the necessary spice and threat to marriage. His function in the plot apart, his character remains sketchily drawn.

We first meet Damian as a traditional courtly lover. Hit by the dart of Venus, he promptly retires to bed, and May comes as the comforting lady, like Criseyde in *Troilus and Criseyde*. As is customary for a courtly lover, he writes a secret letter to his lady, but unlike a traditional mistress, she all too promptly acquiesces to love him. The initiative is thereafter taken over entirely by May, who is responsible for the pear tree plot. January, however, has a high estimation of Damian, calling him

wys, discreet, and as secree
As any man I woot of his degree,
And therto manly, and eek servysable,
And for to been a thrifty man right able.

(R. 1909–12, H. 697–70)

(wise, discerning and as trusty as any man of his rank, and in addition manly and also useful and extremely serviceable.) Later January tells his wife to amuse the sick Damian, as he is 'a gentil man'—that is, noble and worthy. January's estimation of him as trusty, useful and worthy proves to be highly ironic and makes January appear very foolish.

The scene in the tree, when compared to the refined behaviour expected of a courtly lover, shatters the romantic image of May and Damian's love affair. He does indeed appear 'manly', 'discreet' and 'servysable' as far as May is concerned, but, like all the characters in the tale, he is only interested in his own lustful aims, and there is no question of mutual respect or love in the affair. None of the characters, therefore, appears attractive.

A final note of irony is introduced by the name of 'Damian'. St Damian was the patron saint of medicine. We see a man who is love-sick cured by May's agreement to commit adultery, and May's excuse that she was using Damian to cure January's blindness by 'struggling' in a tree with him becomes all the more ironic. The patron saint of medicine does indeed help January to recover his physical sight, but manages to blind him in all other aspects. It is the other Physician who died on the tree, who alone can cure his spiritual blindness.

Part 4

Hints for Study

Reading the text

Chaucer's language seems difficult in the beginning, and much of the difficulty arises because of unfamiliar spelling, vocabulary and word-order. It helps to read the text aloud; then words which are foreign to the eye will be recognised by the ear; for example, 'seyde' (said) and 'trewely' (truly). Reading aloud will also give you a feeling for Chaucer's metre and tone of voice. A couplet such as the following depends on sound:

> That he sholde go biforn with his cliket [key]
> This Damyan thanne hath opened the wyket [gate]
>
> (R. 2151–2, H. 939–40)

The rhymes evoke the sound of a key clicking in a lock. Such poetry was doubtlessly written to be spoken aloud, and much of the humour is lost if it is silently read. Help with difficult vocabulary can be sought in the Notes and Glossaries of these Notes, or in the glossaries of the editions of the tale. It is also strongly recommended that you become familiar with the list of recurrent words on page 65, as there are many common Middle English words that are unfamiliar and therefore slow up your reading. Some are parts of verbs and difficult to find in glossaries, like 'yse' (see) and 'nys' (is not); others are small but important words like 'bet' (better), 'er' (before) or 'syn' (since). The list also contains common Middle English words whose meaning has changed since then; for example, 'nice' (foolish), 'sad' (serious) and 'sely' (good). It is also helpful to look at unfamiliar words in their context, when the sense will often become apparent; for instance, whether 'seyn' means 'since', 'seen' or 'say'.

If a line is difficult to understand, it may be because of unfamiliar word-order, so re-arrange the sentence; for instance, 'And stille he sit under a bussh anon' becomes 'And he immediately sits still under a bush'. Do not be confused by double negative forms; for example, 'Noght for no coveitise' or 'Ther nys no thing in gree superlatyf.' Equally confusing can be the impersonal constructions with the dative; for instance, 'him liste' (he wished) or 'me thinketh' (it seems to me).

The first necessary step is to become familiar with the text and understand the story in detail. Read the text a few times with the help of the Notes and Glossaries until you are fully acquainted with the meaning. You will then be able to appreciate the subtle details and ironies that create the mood that Chaucer wishes to convey. Afterwards the Commentary, Part 3 of these Notes, and the Introduction in the Hussey edition will aid your interpretation of the tale and help you to appreciate such concepts as marriage in the Middle Ages, understand the complex characters of January and the Merchant, and thereby appreciate Chaucer's aim in this tale.

Answering questions

Support your argument with relevant quotations; the selection given on pages 66–8 should help you here, but avoid using quotations as a substitute for argument. You should reach a compromise between stringing together a series of quotations with little commentary and the other extreme, namely, giving insufficient textual evidence. If the quotation is one or two lines long you should incorporate it into your text, like this: 'No man hateth his flessh, but in his lyf/He fostreth it' (lines 174–5). If more than two lines long, centre it on the page.

If you quote or paraphrase from critical works, acknowledge your source and give full bibliographical information. If the quotation from a critical work is longer than two lines, then you should again indent it. Add a list of works you have consulted at the conclusion of your essay, giving full bibliographical information. You can use the bibliography in these Notes as a guide.

Leave plenty of time when you have completed a rough draft of your essay or examination answer to present your findings in a well-constructed essay with a logical argument. Your essay should include an introduction in which your plan and critical methods are outlined and a sound conclusion that sums up your argument.

You will also find it helpful to look at *The Merchant's Tale* in its context in *The Canterbury Tales*, since one of the Merchant's aims is to answer the Wife of Bath and the Clerk. Similar concepts are repeated throughout the tales and your appreciation of Chaucer and medieval thought will be aided by broader reading. Robert P. Miller in *Chaucer, Sources and Background* has collected and translated background material, such as Theophrastus's *The Golden Book of Marriage*.

Recurrent words

There are a number of short, common words in Middle English that often confuse the reader. Many of these have been omitted from the Notes and Glossaries and collected in the following list. It will speed up your reading to become acquainted with these words.

ago: gone
al: all, although
axen: ask
ay: always
ayen: again
been: be; **beth** be
bet: better
bitwix(en): between
chees: chose
cleped: called
dar: dare
dette: debt
doon: do; **dooth:** does *or* do
dostow?: do you?
duren: endure
eek: also
eft: afterwards *or* again
elde: old age
er: before
fader: father
fro: from
ful: very
gan: began; but usually an auxiliary verb to denote past tense
han: have; **hadde:** had; **hath:** has
hem: them
highte: called
hire: her *or* their
holde: consider
hye, heigh: high *or* great
ilke: same
kan: can *or* know; **koude:** could
leten: hinder *or* allow
levere: rather
liketh (hire): (she) likes
list: it pleases
longen: belong
make: mate
maystow: may you
mo: more
morwe: morrow
moste, moot: must
muchel: much

myn: my
nas: was not; **nys:** is not
ne: not, nor
nice: foolish
nolde: would not
o, oon: one
paraunter: perhaps
quod: said
sad: serious
saugh, say: saw; **seyn:** seen
sely: innocent, good
seye: say; **seith:** says; **seyn:** to say; **seyde:** said
seyn: since *or* say *or* seen
shaltow?: shall you?
sith: since
soothly: truly; **sooth:** true
spak: spoke
stant: stands
swich: such
syn: since
than(ne): then
thilke: that
tho: those *or* then
thurgh: through
thyn: your
verray: true
-we suffixes: '-ow', e.g. **sorwe:** sorrow; **folwe:** follow
wenen: to think *or* imagine
whan: when
wight: person
witen: to know; **woot:** knows
wole: will; **wolde:** would
woxen: becomes
yaf: gave; **yeven:** to give; **yeveth:** gives
ye: you
yen: eyes
ynogh: enough
yoore: long ago
yse: see
y- prefix: indicates the past participle, e.g. **ybroght:** brought

Some key quotations

(1) The Merchant's views on his marriage can be illustrated by this quotation:

> I have a wyf, the worste that may be;
> For thogh the feend to hire ycoupled were,
> She wolde hym overmacche, I dar wel swere.
>
> (R. 1218–20, H. 6–8)

(2) January's idealized view of marriage is quite different:

> 'Noon oother lyf,' seyde he, 'is worth a bene;
> For wedlok is so esy and so clene,
> That in this world it is a paradys.'
>
> (R. 1263–5, H. 51–3)

(3) January paraphrases the medieval attitude to marriage in this way:

> If he ne may nat lyven chaast his lyf,
> Take hym a wyf with greet devocioun,
> By cause of leveful procreacioun
> Of children, to th'onour of God above,
> And nat oonly for paramour or love;
> And for they sholde leccherye eschue,
> And yelde hir dette whan that it is due;
>
> (R. 1446–52, H. 234–40)

(4) Justinus's views on marriage echo those of the Merchant:

> For, God it woot, I have wept many a teere
> Ful pryvely, syn I have had a wyf.
> Preyse whoso wole a wedded mannes lyf,
> Certein I fynde in it but cost and care
> And observances, of alle blisses bare.
>
> (R. 1544–8, H. 332–6)

(5) References to marriage as Heaven, Purgatory or Hell on earth are as follows:

(*a*) See line R. 1265, H. 53, quoted above.

(*b*) That wyf is mannes helpe and his confort,
His paradys terrestre, and his disport.

> (R. 1331–2, H. 119–20)

(*c*) *January*: '. . . I shal have myn hevene in erthe heere.'

> (R. 1647, H. 435)

(*d*) And Januarie hath faste in armes take
His fresshe May, his paradys, his make.

> (R. 1821–2, H. 609 –10)

(e) *Justinus*: 'Paraunter she may be youre purgatorie!'

(R. 1670, H. 458)

(f) The narrator will not say 'wheither hire thoughte it paradys or helle' when January embraces May.

(R. 1964, H. 752)

(6) May's attitude to January is implied by silence:

The bryde was broght abedde as stille as stoon;

(R. 1818, H. 606)

But God woot what that May thoughte in hir herte,
Whan she hym saugh up sittynge in his sherte
In his nyght-cappe, and with his nekke lene;
She preyseth nat his pleyyng worth a bene.

(R. 1851–4, H. 639–42)

(7) Chaucer strengthens the distasteful portrait of January in the vivid bedroom scene:

He lulleth hire, he kisseth hire ful ofte;
With thikke brustles of his berd unsofte,
Lyk to the skyn of houndfyssh, sharp as brere

(R. 1823–5, H. 611–13)

The slakke skyn about his nekke shaketh,
Whil that he sang, so chaunteth he and craketh.

(R. 1849–50, H. 637–8)

(8) An example of the narrator's exaggerated rhetorical outbursts is his attack on Fortune; here is the opening:

O sodeyn hap! o thou Fortune unstable!
Lyk to the scorpion so deceyvable,
That flaterest with thyn heed whan thou wolt stynge;

(R. 2057–9, H. 845–7)

(9) Here is January's mock paraphrase of The Song of Solomon:

'Rys up, my wyf, my love, my lady free!
The turtles voys is herd, my dowve sweete;
The wynter is goon with alle his reynes weete.
Com forth now, with thyne eyen columbyn!
How fairer been thy brestes than is wyn!
The gardyn is enclosed al aboute;'

(R. 2138–43, H. 926–31)

(10) Finally, here is the scene of revelation when January's sight is restored:

Up to the tree he caste his eyen two,
And saugh that Damyan his wyf had dressed
In swich manere it may nat been expressed,
But if I wolde speke uncurteisly;
And up he yaf a roryng and a cry.

(R. 2360−4, H. 1148−52)

Some questions and guidelines to answers

What is the significance of the Pluto and Proserpina episode?

First discuss the dramatic function of introducing new characters at
such a late point in the tale. This interpolation causes suspense by
creating a deliberately frustrating interruption in the otherwise fast-
moving fabliau. Being mythical characters with supernatural powers,
they can also bring about a miraculous cure.

You could then find out as much as possible about the mythological
Pluto and Proserpina (Hades and Persephone in Greek myth). Such
information can be found in a dictionary of classical mythology, while
brief accounts are given in the Commentary part of these Notes and in
the introduction to Hussey's edition, where there is an outline of the
version of the tale Chaucer used, namely Claudius Claudianus's *De
Raptu Proserpinae*. You would then be able to compare Pluto and
January and Proserpina and May—for instance, the men's blindness,
old age, riches, selfish love and oppression of a young girl, and the
women's eloquence, fertility associations, youth and clever escape
from dominant husbands. The locations they inhabit are also significant: the hell of the marriage bed and the spring-like garden where
May meets the love of her choice. The parallels are discussed in greater
detail in the Commentary. It would also be necessary to analyse the
characters of Pluto and Proserpina as presented in this tale, and the
significance of Pluto's anti-feminism which parallels the views of
Justinus and probably of the Merchant himself.

The major part of such an answer should involve a discussion of the
significance of these parallels: the two husbands' blindness to mutual
love and respect in marriage, their covetousness in wishing to imprison
young girls in their respective kingdoms, and the women's abuse of
eloquence to deceive their husbands. Conclusions could be drawn concerning the attitudes to marriage that this episode underlines, the significance of the fertile garden and the theme of the marriage of wisdom
and eloquence which is discussed in the Commentary. The contrast
between richly fertile setting and spiritually barren characters can also
be drawn, as well as the comparison between this garden and Eden.

Such a question could lead on to a general discussion of the Merchant's aim in his tale of stressing the deceits of women, an aim which is greatly helped by this apparent interpolation.

Discuss the different attitudes to love and marriage presented in this tale.

The list of quotations given above will help you to give textual evidence for the different views on marriage found in the tale. There is the lustful attitude to love and marriage found in January and Damian, the economic attitude that January, May and probably the Merchant share, and the anti-matrimonial views put forward by Pluto and Justinus.

A good starting-point could be the official view of the church on marriage. You could consult a prayer book of one of the Christian denominations; the contemporary Anglican one mentions the symbolic union of Christ and Holy Church and the major reasons for marriage that January lists. The sections in the Commentary on 'Love and Marriage', 'Courtly Love' and 'The Church's Views on Marriage' should also help. Having established the orthodox views, you could then show how January manipulates them for his own lustful purposes.

The anti-feminist and anti-matrimonial views are presented by Justinus and Pluto. Background information can be found in Robert P. Miller's *Chaucer, Sources and Background*, pages 397–493. This work also contains the marriage vows (page 374) as found in the *Sarum Missal*.

Illicit love, of course, can be illustrated by the conduct of May and Damian. You could present the theory behind the concept of Courtly Love, which you can find in the 'Courtly Love' section of the Commentary; and in Miller's work there is a translation of part of Andreas Capellanus's *Treatise on Love*. Once more the difference between theory and practice can be stressed by comparing the ideal with the reality found in this tale.

Finally you might like to extract examples from the tale that show the economic aspects of marriage; the way January treats the event as a business deal and May as his own property. The conclusions will probably be that none of the forms of male-female relationship discussed in this tale is applauded by Chaucer.

To what extent can this tale be called a fabliau?

First you need to define what is meant by a fabliau; you might mention that it is a tale told by a 'low' character, including realistic and dramatic action, crude behaviour and of course humour. The plot that centres on an old husband, a young wife and her lover is very common in this tradition. Help concerning the nature of the fabliau can be sought in the section on 'Genre and Style' in the Commentary. Once you have established what is expected in this genre, you can then discuss the fabliau elements in *The Merchant's Tale*. The central story of the pear tree can be extracted and the fast-moving action, crude details, colloquial speech, economy of language and so on, shown to be typical of this genre. You might even like to compare this tale with *The Miller's Tale* or another fabliau in *The Canterbury Tales* in order to stress the similarities.

However, there is much in the tale that does not conform with the fabliau genre, especially in the first part, which is more like a sermon or a debate. Moreover, the Pluto and Proserpina interlude is not typical of the fast-moving fabliau. And there are lofty rhetorical speeches, such as the exclamations concerning deceitful servants and fortune. Such eloquence on the part of the Merchant changes a crude, basic story into what would appear a well-argued debate. The form of the tale, therefore, reflects the teller; it suits Chaucer's aim of showing a deceitful person, the Merchant, using his gifts of eloquence to convince us that all marriages are disastrous and all wives deceitful.

It is particularly helpful to analyse the way in which January debates: he presents both sides of the argument for and against marriage and uses the orthodox Christian view to support his enthusiasm for the state of matrimony, yet invariably undercuts himself by letting his true reasons slip out—namely to continue his lecherous life under the cloak of respectability. He gets his friends to give advice, but is as deaf to those who disagree as he is blind to the true significance of marriage or to his own self-delusion. The initial section and all the rhetorical devices, then, prove unnecessary as far as January's decision is concerned. He is as blind at the beginning as he is at the end. These lofty additions to the fabliau simply reflect the teller and his deceitful aims. Genre and style are therefore of major importance to the central theme.

Part 5

Suggestions for further reading

The text

ROBINSON, F.N. (ED.): *The Works of Geoffrey Chaucer*, Oxford University Press, London, second edition, 1957. This is the standard edition of Chaucer's complete works and has sufficient notes and glossary.

HUSSEY, MAURICE (ED.): *The Merchant's Prologue and Tale*, Selected Tales from Chaucer, Cambridge University Press, Cambridge, 1966. This is the most useful edition of the individual tale and contains a good introduction, notes and glossary.

CAWLEY, A.C. (ED.): *Chaucer: The Canterbury Tales*, Everyman's Library, Dent, London, 1958. As this edition has an on-the-page glossary, it is good for rapid reading, but notes will still be needed.

General works

BREWER, D.S.: *Chaucer in his Time*, Longman, London, 1973. An excellent background work on Chaucer.

DAVIS, N.: *A Chaucer Glossary*, Oxford University Press, Oxford, 1979.

HUSSEY, MAURICE: *Chaucer's World, A Pictorial Guide*, Cambridge University Press, Cambridge, 1967. Contains useful background information and excellent illustrations.

MILLER, ROBERT P.: *Chaucer, Sources and Background*, Oxford University Press, New York, 1977. The translations of source material, such as anti-matrimonial literature, are useful.

Critical works

BLANCH, ROBERT J. (ED.): *Geoffrey Chaucer: The Merchant's Tale*, Charles E. Merrill, Ohio, 1970. Contains an excellent collection of critical essays on this tale.

BREWER, D.S.: *Chaucer*, Longman, London, 1973.

DONALDSON, E.T.: *Speaking of Chaucer*, Athlone Press, London, 1970.

HOWARD, D.R.: *The Idea of The Canterbury Tales*, University of California Press, Berkeley, Cal., 1976.

HUSSEY, S.S.: *An Introduction to Chaucer*, Methuen, London, 1971.

RUGGIERS, PAUL G.: *The Art of The Canterbury Tales*, University of Wisconsin Press, Madison, *Wisconsin*, 1965.

WHITTOCK, T.: *A Reading of The Canterbury Tales*, Cambridge University Press, Cambridge, 1970.

The author of these notes

GRAHAM D. CAIE is senior lecturer in the English Department of the University of Copenhagen where he teaches medieval English literature. His publications include *The Judgment Day Theme in Old English Poetry* and a number of articles on the significance of early glosses in the manuscripts of *The Canterbury Tales*. His special interest is inter-disciplinary teaching and research in the Middle Ages. At present he is completing a critical edition of the Old English *Judgment Day II* poem.